THE PERFECT DATE...OR NOT

"Things are looking up for a change," I told our cat as I flipped off all the lights but one and settled into my makeshift bed for the night. Davide sauntered over and jumped up on me so he could sleep on my hip. "Not even a missing horse and half-naked Viking ghosts running around are going to ruin my date with Ben day after tomorrow. That is going to be the most perfect event of my life, I just know it."

Which just goes to show you I'm *not* clairvoyant in any way.

CIRCUS
OF THE
DARNED

KATIE MAXWELL

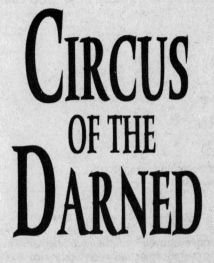

SMOOCH NEW YORK CITY

*A thousand and one fervent thank-yous
go to my friend Tobias Barlind (also known as Coldshark),
who generously allowed me to pester him for extremely odd
Swedish phrases. Tackar så mycket, Sharky!*

SMOOCH ®

January 2006

Published by

Dorchester Publishing Co., Inc.
200 Madison Avenue
New York, NY 10016

ISBN 0-8439-5400-0

Visit us on the web at www.smoochya.com.

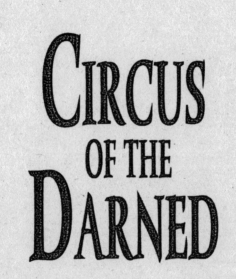

CIRCUS
OF THE
DARNED

CHAPTER ONE

"Good morning, Fran."

"Morning, Tallulah. How's Sir Edward?"

Tallulah smiled a sad smile. "Still dead, alas."

I nodded, not surprised at all by her answer. According to what Tallulah, a medium of gypsy ancestry, had told me a couple of months before, Sir Edward had been dead for a few hundred years. It didn't stop him from being her boyfriend, but I didn't have the nerve to ask just what sort of a relationship was possible with a ghost.

I wandered down the line of trailers that housed the members of the GothFaire, musing on the fact that in a short time, I'd come pretty far.

"*Guten morgen*, Francesca."

"Morning, Kurt." It was hard to believe, but just two months ago, Mom had to drag me kicking and screaming to Europe to spend the next six months with her while my father had time to "get to know" his new trophy wife. What was harder to believe was that I would find an odd sense of companionship with members of the GothFaire . . . a stranger group of people I couldn't imagine.

"Ah, Fran. It is you." A slight woman with spiky pink hair appeared in the trailer's doorway behind the big, blond Kurt (according to Faire gossip, both Kurt and his brother Karl had a thing going with Absinthe).

"Sure is. Morning, Absinthe." I gave her a friendly smile that I didn't really mean, and hurried on my way before she could say anything else.

"Vait a moment! I vish to speaks with you . . ."

"Sorry, have to feed Tesla. Maybe later!" I called over my shoulder, silently swearing at the unhappy frown she fired off at me. The last thing I needed was to tick off the woman who ran the Faire, but no way was I going to let her pin me down again. Ever since she'd found out about my special power, she'd been after me to do a mind-reading act . . . something I intended to avoid like the plague.

"*Tja*, Fran."

"*Hej, god morgon*," I answered politely. I figured since we were in Sweden, I should at least learn a little of the language. Tibolt stood outside his trailer in a tank top and a pair of sweats and did some stretches before his morning run. I stopped, unable to keep my feet moving. "Um. *Hur mår du? Allt väl?*"

Tibolt smiled, and I swear, the birds started singing louder. From behind me, I heard a loud gasp, then the sound of feet racing toward us. "I am fine, everything is good, and your Swedish is improving greatly."

"*Tack*," I thanked him, trying to stop the Inner Fran

lt.
air
a
ut
to
es,
h-
n-
?"
ld
g,
he
de
e-
o-
a
no
is-
he
g,
d-

"Hmm?"

meadow and

cus of the Da

the causeway

which made

wonder if he i

"Whose pre

bumps that h

"No one im

ladies. I was t

have a favor to

"Favor? Su

me, Imogen t

"I would be

said, looking

Tibolt flash

her fall down

Fran can help

smile on me,

safe with you

I stiffened

face. "The wh

Tibolt pulle

On it hung a

intertwined tr

of the Viking

"A *Viking*

sort of Swedi

He nodded

The pendant

body heat. I g

the pendant, partly from Tibolt being so close to me. "That is it exactly. A valknut is the knot of the slain, a symbol of eternity and the afterlife. You see the nine points on it?"

I touched the three triangles. The pendant felt nice, kind of tingly, like it hummed with power of its own. "Yeah."

"They represent the three Norns, the weavers of fates."

"Fate weavers. OK. Um . . . why are you giving me this?"

He smiled. Imogen sucked in her breath again. "I need it kept safe for me tonight. You can wear it under your shirt while you read palms. It won't interfere with your reading. In fact, it may even help you."

I touched the pendant again. Imogen made an envious sort of noise, so I held it up for her to touch, as well.

"It's lovely," she said, stroking one of the points. "Is it old?"

"Very. It was my grandfather's, and his before him on back for as many generations as my family has existed. And now, I must be on my morning run, or I will not have time to prepare the hallowed ground for the *blot*." He stretched both arms above his head. Imogen froze, clutching my arm, her eyes huge as she watched him.

"You're going to prepare a bloat?" I asked, glancing at Imogen. Her mouth hung open a little. I elbowed her until she closed it.

"Yes. A *blot* is a ritual sacrifice we in the Asatru make as an offering to the gods." Tibolt did two hamstring stretches that had Imogen gurgling, and me clutching the side of the trailer.

"Um," I said, desperate to distract myself from him. I knew the Asatru religion honored ancient Nordic gods. But I'd never heard of a *blot*. "Don't ritual sacrifices involve killing sweet little innocent animals?"

"In the old days, they did," he said, nodding as he did calf stretches. "But now we use mead instead of blood. It is much more pleasant that way. See you later." He took off before we could ask him how you ritually sacrificed a glass of wine with honey.

Imogen and I stood together, our eyes glued to the figure of the blond hottie as he trotted around the line of trailers and headed to the other side of the island, toward the ruins of a Viking fortress.

"He is the most gorgeous creature I have ever seen," Imogen said in an awestruck voice.

I dragged my eyes from the disappearing figure of Tibolt (which wasn't easy) to look at Imogen, and giggled at the googly-eyed look of utter besottedness on her face, even though I had a horrible suspicion I wore the very same expression. "Yeah, he's pretty all that and a bag of chips, but as Soren says, he's just a guy, you know?"

"Soren?" Imogen said, making a ladylike snort. Everything Imogen did was ladylike. Even now, having just gotten up and accepted the latte that Peter, Soren's father, had brought her, she looked gorgeous. Long curly blond hair, a fashion sense that made me feel like I was forever wearing a garbage bag, and delicate, pretty features would probably be enough to make me hate her on sight if she had been a normal person, but Imogen was anything but normal.

Which more or less described everyone here at the Faire.

"Yeah, I know, he's only a kid, but sometimes he sees stuff better than other people."

She released my wrist, smiled, and patted me on the shoulder. "Soren is only a year younger than you, Fran. That hardly makes him a little kid."

I lifted my chin and gave her one of my "I'm confident" smiles that I've been practicing when I'm alone in our trailer. "Yeah, but there's a big difference between fifteen and sixteen. I've killed a demon, and figured out who an international thief was. Not to mention that whole vampire business."

"Dark One," she corrected automatically, taking a sip of her latte as she turned back toward her trailer.

"Sorry, Dark One. Anyway, I doubt that I could have done all that last year without having a major panic attack. Fifteen can be so, you know . . . *fifteen*."

"Mmm." She didn't look impressed. In fact, she changed the subject. "Speaking of Benedikt, he should be here soon."

I had started waking toward the field beyond the horse trailer, where Bruno, the horse that Peter used in his magic act, and Tesla, my bought-on-a-whim elderly horse, grazed. But at Imogen's words, I spun around. "What? You've heard from him? Where is he? What happened to him? Why did he leave so quickly, without any explanation, just a note saying there was something important he had to do, and he didn't know when he'd be back? And why didn't he tell one of us where he'd gone?"

Imogen shrugged and kept walking. "I haven't heard from him directly, but I can feel that he's near. I'm sure he'll answer all your questions once he returns." She gave me an amused glance over her shoulder. "You are, after all, his Beloved. He can't lie to you."

"Hrmph," I answered to no one in particular, heading back to where the horses grazed, pausing long enough to snatch up the nylon lead. "I'm beginning to believe that whole Beloved thing is more trouble than its worth. If Ben really thought I was the only person on the face of the earth who could save his soul, you'd think he'd be a little more chatty about where he's been for the last three weeks, and what he's been doing, and why he hasn't called or sent a letter or anything."

Tesla wickered softly and shoved his big horsey nose against my stomach as I approached, looking for a treat. I undid the leather hobble that connected his front legs and kept him from wandering. Not that I seriously thought he'd run off. I had rescued him from a knacker while we were in Hungary, and though I didn't know much about his history, I knew he was too old to go far. But Peter insisted that the horses be hobbled while they were grazing at night. "Yeah, yeah, hold on a moment, will you? Here. Apple. It's the best I could do."

Tesla's gray whiskers tickled my palm as he snuffled the apple that lay across my hand. He decided to accept the offering, carefully plucking it off my hand, munching it happily while I snapped the lead on his halter, and led him toward the trailer. As we walked, I slipped my hand under his mane and touched the raised marking on his neck. Ben had said it was a brand and that all Lipizzans, a very special breed of horse, had them. Since Ben had lived for more than three hundred years, and learned a lot about horses during that time, I figured he had to know what he was talking about. "Although that doesn't mean he's not the most irritating guy in the world," I told Tesla as we halted behind the horse trailer. "Going off without a word to anyone like that . . ."

"Talking to yourself?" Soren limped around the trailer, two buckets of grain in his hands. I tied Tesla next to Bruno, a glossy white Andalusian, and made yet another mental promise to give Tesla a bath. It wasn't that Tesla was dirty, but next to Bruno's glossy coat he was more of a grayish color than pure white.

"No, I'm talking to Tesla."

Soren's eyebrows scrunched up as he handed me a bucket. "Same difference. I bet you were talking about *him* again."

I fed and watered Tesla, waiting until Soren was done pampering Bruno before grabbing his sleeve and tugging him toward the blue-and-gold trailer I shared with my mother. "Come on, my mom is cooking breakfast."

"Really? She's cooking?"

"Yeah, I know, a miracle, huh? Think I should call the newspapers or something?"

Soren snickered. We both waved at Mikaela and Ramon as they emerged from their Circus of the Darned RV looking sleepy.

"Why is she cooking?" Soren asked. "You didn't cast one of her own spells on her, did you?"

I laughed. "Mom is the witch, not me. I'm just . . ." I held up my gloved hands, the black lace outer gloves hiding the fact that beneath them I wore a thin, flesh-colored pair of latex gloves. "She's making breakfast as penance."

"Ah," he said, nodding his head wisely. I fought to keep a smile from curling my lips. Soren was the only one near my age in the whole GothFaire, so we tended to hang out together a lot. Besides which, he was my friend. He helped me with Tesla, and he tried to teach me the magic tricks he was learning from his father, although I didn't seem to have his knack for it. "She lost her keys again?"

"Cell phone," I answered. "The new one she just bought to cover all of Europe."

"Ah," he said again, and this time I did grin. I thought he'd grin back, but instead he shot me a serious, half-wary look from beneath the thick brown lock of hair that hung over his forehead. "What did you say to Tesla?"

"What did I say . . . oh. Just now? Nothing important."

Soren sucked on his bottom lip for a moment, before saying quickly, "You were talking about *him*, weren't you?"

"Him who?" I asked, knowing exactly whom he was talking about.

"Benedikt." He rolled his eyes as he hurried alongside me. I slowed down a hair, remembering that he couldn't walk as fast as I could. "He's the only one who makes you get that look on your face."

"What look?" I touched my gloved fingertips to my face.

His brows pulled together in a frown. "The one you get around Benedikt—kind of dreamy, kind of annoyed."

I laughed out loud. I couldn't help myself—Soren's description of my expression just about perfectly described my reaction to Ben, vampire of my dreams. Or so he wanted to be. I still wasn't sure about the whole girlfriend to a Moravian Dark One thing. "I wish you'd lighten up on Ben, Soren. He's not really as bad as he looks."

"He has a motorcycle and long hair," Soren said darkly, his freckled fair-skinned face going red with embarassment. He refused to meet my eyes as I socked him gently on the arm. "And earrings and tattoos. And he makes you angry sometimes."

"A lot of people have long hair, motorcycles, earrings, tats, and make me angry," I said, caught between the desire to tell Soren the truth about Ben, and the urge to tell him there was nothing going on between us. Because of his physical defect (one leg was a few inches shorter than the other), Soren tended to be a bit touchy sometimes, especially concerning Ben. I don't quite know why he'd taken such an instant dislike to Ben, but I did my best to keep him from getting too bent out of shape. "He just happens to be one of them. And before you say it, I know he's dangerous, you don't trust him, and he means only trouble for me. Heard it before, got the T-shirt, Soren."

He made an angry sniffing noise as we rounded the long metal trailer that Mom had let me paint when we arrived at GothFaire two months before. Everyone's trailer had been customized to reflect their personality, and ours was, I thought, a particularly nice arrangement of gold stars and moons on a midnight blue background.

I admired it for a moment before I realized that Soren wasn't saying anything.

I sighed to myself, knowing that I'd inadvertently offended him. "I'm sorry, Soren. I didn't mean to make you mad. I appreciate you being all concerned about Ben, but honest, there's no reason to be. We're just friends. And he's not going to do anything to hurt me. He can't, he's . . ." I closed my mouth over the words that would spill Ben's secret. As far as I knew, only two people in the GothFaire other than Imogen and I knew what she and Ben really were. I wasn't about to go blabbing around to everyone that they were part of an immortal race that most people thought of as vampires.

"I'm not mad," he said stiffly. "I don't care what you do."

I stopped Soren as he was about to walk past the door to our trailer, my hand on his arm. He looked down at my gloves, his eyes stormy. I gritted my teeth for a moment, then peeled off both the black lace glove and the latex one, gently touching my fingertips to his wrist. Instantly my head was filled with his emotions, anger roiling around with frustration, a smidgen of jealousy, and something soft and warm, a squidgy feeling of . . . I gasped and jerked my hand back. Soren's cheeks fired up even redder than they had become with just a few days in the strong Swedish sunlight, but his eyes didn't leave mine, almost belligerantly daring me to say what I'd felt within him.

"Oh. I . . . uh . . ." I stammered, not knowing what to say. I slipped my gloves back on, waving toward the trailer door. "We'd better hurry to breakfast while Mom is still in the cooking mood."

He stiffened for a minute, and I thought he was going to say something, but instead he gave a sharp little nod and swung open the door to the trailer.

I blew out a breath I didn't realize I'd been holding and followed him, wondering how it was that just two months ago I'd wanted to blend into the crowd, praying that no one would notice that I was different from everyone else in my high school. Big, gawky, and uncomfortable around the kids in my school because of my weird talent, I had few friends and not much of a life. Now here I was traveling all over Europe with a job—palm reader in training—a horse that depended on me to earn his feed and vet bills, a drop-dead gorgeous vampire claiming I was the person he'd waited three hundred years for, and Soren crushing like mad on me.

Life is sometimes too weird for words.

CHAPTER TWO

"Oh, there you are. How did the readings go tonight, honey?"

I shrugged and slipped behind my mother into the booth, where she handed out spells and bottles of good luck, protective amulets of all varieties, and her big seller, love charms. "Same old, same old. Big and small mounds of Mars, lots of lines, a couple of scars, and one missing finger."

She gave me a warning look out of the corner of one eye as I picked up Davide, her fat black-and-white cat, and sat down in the chair he'd been occupying. Davide gave me a long look, his whiskers twitching irritably as I stroked his back. Mom handed over a bottle of good luck, warning the buyer to use it sparingly.

"Were you wearing your gloves?" she asked, once the buyer had trotted off. "Or did you really read palms?"

I lifted my chin. Mom had made a deal with Peter that I would read palms every night for four hours, in exchange for Tesla's food and other incidentals. Peter said once my apprenticeship to Imogen was up—I had another two months left on that—he'd also start paying me a salary in addition to the horsey things. "I did the readings the only way I know how."

She shook her head as she gathered up her things. "Franny, Franny, Franny . . . the god and goddess gave you a gift. You should be proud of it, proud to use it to help people."

"I don't see how being able to feel people's emotions and thoughts is going to help anyone—"

"You were given that gift for a reason, honey," she said, just like I knew she would. We'd had this argument regularly since I was twelve, when my "gift" (I thought of it as a curse) manifested itself. "If you would just open yourself up to the path . . . oh, bullfrogs, I'm late. I'm off to get into my invocation things. We're short on happiness and insight, honey, so don't allow anyone to buy more than one of each."

I nodded, eyeing the colorful array of glass vials that Mom had set out to entice buyers. Unlike other people who hocked similar items, the stuff my mother made and sold actually worked. I know, I had a case of the giggles for three weeks straight last year after she accidently spilled a batch of happiness on me.

"Oh, there's a man looking for you," she called over her shoulder as she hurried off toward our trailer. She waved toward the end of the row of booths, where the main tent that held the magic shows was located. "I think he's somewhere down there."

"A man?" I asked, wondering if Ben had returned. But no, Mom knew Ben. Even if she didn't approve of him—and I sensed another "you're too young to have a boyfriend" lecture coming over her—she wouldn't refer to him as just *a man*. I wondered who could be looking for me, and why, but didn't have too long to ponder the question. Mom's booth was very popular no matter what country we were in because she used only positive magic.

"I'm sorry, but for curses, you'll have to visit the de-monologist," I politely told a serious-looking young man. I held up an onyx-colored bottle decorated with a question mark charm. "The nastiest thing we have here is forgetfulness."

The man frowned even more. "Where is this demonologist?"

I pointed toward the right. Although it was almost eleven o'clock at night, it was still light out, kind of a twi-light. Because we were so far north, the sun never completely set during the summer. The Swedes have something they call white nights—basically, it's light enough to read by, but not as bright as the midnight sun areas farther north in the Arctic Circle. "Black and white–striped awning on the left-hand side. His name is Armand. You can't miss him—he has a goatee and horns."

The man blinked at me.

"The horns are fake," I reassured him. "Just for effect." I waited before the guy left before adding, "At least I *think* they're fake."

You never really knew with the people around here.

I sold a few spells, had to argue with a lady who wanted to buy all three of the remaining bottles of inner beauty, and caught someone trying to do the five-finger discount on a packet of dried rose petals (one of the ingredients in the do-it-yourself love spell kit). I've always told Mom that she should keep something bad on hand for people who tried to rip her off, but she insists that we return cruelty with kindness, so instead of calling over Kurt (who, in addition to being a magician, also doubled as a security guy), I grabbed the girl's hand and sprinkled a little kindness on it, gritting my teeth the whole time.

"Have you seen Tib?" Mikaela asked when the shoplifting girl ran off rubbing her hand. She stopped in front of the booth, scanning the crowds.

"Not lately, but if you look for a group of drooling women, you're bound to find him," I answered, sucking in my lips in case I was slobbering just thinking about Tibolt.

Mikaela, her husband Ramon, and Tibolt made up Circus of the Darned, a group that specialized in odd sideshow-type acts. C of D was traveling with us for a couple weeks, something they evidently did each year.

Mikaela made an annoyed sound, her short black hair sticking up like a porcupine's spines. She muttered something in Swedish, then said, "He is supposed to be checking the chainsaws!"

"The chainsaws? Oh, for your juggling bit. Yeah, well, you know Tibolt. Where he goes, so go a whole bunch of girls."

Mikaela, who just happened to be Tibolt's cousin, rolled her kohl-lined eyes. "Hrmph. When is your mother's circle?"

"In an hour. She always holds them at midnight. Something to do with the lineup of stars and stuff. Are you going to watch?"

"No, she has invited me to join."

My eyebrows raised up. Mom was usually very picky about inviting non-witches to participate in her circles. She normally tapped into the big Wiccan network that spread across Europe, using the local witches to form circles.

"Are you Wiccan?" I asked.

Her spiky hair trembled as she shook her head. "I am a high priestess of Ashtar."

"Wow. A high priestess who juggles running chainsaws, spews fire, and swallows swords. Cool!"

She grinned at me for a minute. "It runs in my family. Tibolt is a mage, you know, but he will be at the *blot* tonight after our show."

"He's a mage?"

She nodded. "A practitioner of magic. He is fifth level."

I couldn't help wondering if he was working some sort of mojo that had all the girls fawning on him. I mean, yeah, he was gorgeous and all, but I had a seriously hot guy who believed that I was the key to his salvation, and yet even I couldn't resist staring at Tibolt.

"Uh . . . how many levels of mageness are there?"

"Seven. Oh, there he is—I will see you at the circle, yes?"

I sighed. "Probably. Mom likes me to watch. She thinks it's good for my inner spirit or something like that."

She mumbled something about that being true, then raced off toward the tall blond man who was being swarmed by a gaggle of females.

Ten minutes later I was relieved of booth duty, and went off to watch the end of Peter and Soren's magic act.

Normally the magic acts were over by ten PM so whatever Goth band was playing with us that week could set up and go live by eleven, but the during the two weeks that Circus of the Darned teamed up with the Faire, there were no bands, and the magic acts alternated with C of D shows, which included a killer double sword–swallowing finale that made me hold my breath.

I slipped into the back of the main tent, standing at the rear to avoid getting in anyone's way. When you're almost six feet tall and built like a linebacker, you tend to block people's views. On the raised stage, Peter and Soren were turning a member of the audience into Bruno. That was an illusion, of course, not the real magic that Peter sometimes did, the kind that left my arms covered in goose bumps. I rubbed my arms just thinking about it, hoping that tonight he would feel inspired enough to perform one of his mind-boggling magic tricks.

". . . and with the magic words—what were they?" Peter waited for the crowd to shout back the magic words, which were never the same.

"Isosceles triangle!" the audience shouted in response.

I smiled. Peter told me two nights before he was running out of magic words, and did I have any suggestions for words that had a nice alliteration. Evidently he was as desperate as he said, because I didn't think my suggestion sounded particularly magical or alliterative, but the crowd seemed to get a kick out of it.

"I say the magic words—*isosceles triangle*—and voilà! Jan has been turned into a wild stallion."

Soren whipped off the thin nylon covering the metal frame that hid Bruno from the audience's view. The horse charged down the stage, stopping at the edge to rear on his back legs and paw the air as if he were about to leap straight into the audience. People shrieked and threw themselves down, some laughing, some yelling exclamations at the thought of a dangerous horse loose.

It was all an act, of course. Bruno was very well trained, so well trained that I'd never seen him put a hoof wrong. I watched him paw the air, the sight of it triggering a memory of something Tesla had done a few weeks before, when a demon had attacked us.

Why do you look so puzzled? a soft voice asked next to me.

"What Bruno's doing . . . I think Tesla did the same thing. That move where he sits on his haunches and paws the air—"

It suddenly struck me that the voice I had heard had spoken directly into my mind. And there was only one person I knew who could do that.

Ben?

Right behind you.

I spun around to see Ben lounging in the doorway of the tent, wearing a cool Indiana Jones–type hat, and the same black leather motorcycle jacket I'd seen him in before. His arms were crossed over his chest, a kind of half-smile on his face as he watched me. My stomach did a funny little flip-flop as I smiled back at him. I forgot for a minute that I was mad at him for taking off without telling me, instead wanting to just look at him.

Tesla is a Lipizzan. I told you that.

Huh? I was a bit confused by why he was talking about Tesla for a moment. *Oh, yeah, you did. So?*

The move Bruno made is called a levade.

A le-what?

Levade. It's one of the airs above the ground.

I walked over to where Ben leaned against the door frame. "Hi. What's an air above the ground?"

"A series of movements that Lipizzans are known for."

"OK. But Bruno isn't a Lipizzan."

"No, he isn't, but he's related to them. Andalusians are occasionally trained in the airs above the ground as well."

"Huh." I said, then socked him on the shoulder. Hard. "Where the horned bullfrogs have you been? And why haven't you called? Or sent me an e-mail or a letter or something? Why did you disappear like that, without a word to anyone? I thought you wanted to do the boyfriend thing with me?"

"What boyfriend thing would that be?" he asked, looking at my mouth. My stomach did three backflips in a row. "Are you talking about kissing? Did you want to practice on me some more?"

If my stomach had been in the Olympics, it would have won a medal for gymnastics. I stared at Ben's mouth, feeling incredibly squidgy, but at the same time,

I couldn't look away. Ben was the world's best kisser—he'd had more than three hundred years to practice, so that was no surprise—but what *was* a surprise was how much I enjoyed his lessons.

Don't get me wrong, I've never had anything against guys. They're, you know, guys. Nice sometimes, sometimes not. But I've never really wanted to kiss one of them the way I wanted to kiss Ben.

"Fran? Do you want to kiss me?"

"Yeah," I answered, then remembered an episode of Ricki Lake that said guys like it when you play hard to get. Something about the thrill of the chase. "I mean, no. Maybe. Er . . . what was the question?"

He laughed and pulled me outside the tent, into the shadow of the ticket booth, his hands warm around my waist. *I prefer you enthusiastic and willing rather than hard to get. Say Mississippi.*

"I have a better place name," I whispered against his lips. "It's the name of a town in Wales."

And that would be . . . ?

"Llanfairpwllgwyngyllgogerychwyrndrobwyllllantysili-ogogogoch," I murmured, my lips against his in a way that made all my insides melt into a great big puddle.

He laughed into my head.

What, did I say it wrong? I memorized the pronunciation from a Web site.

I don't know if the pronunciation is correct or not; all I know is I like how you say it.

I let him kiss me then, *really* kiss me, because . . . well, he was good at it. And even though I was pissed at him,

I wasn't so pissed I didn't want to kiss him, so I just kept whispering the Llanfairpwyll word (it's easier to pronounce than it looks).

"Miss Ghetti?" A soft voice followed by an embarrassed cough managed to work its way through my brain. "My apologies for disturbing you, but are you Miss Francesca Ghetti? The owner of the horse currently grazing in the meadow next to the fortress?"

Ben spun around and blocked my view of the man who spoke. "Who are you?"

I shoved his back, but he didn't move, so I edged my way around him, blushing like mad that someone had caught Ben and me lip wrestling. "Hi. I'm Fran."

"What do you want her for?" Ben asked.

I pinched his wrist, smiling at the man in front of me. He didn't look like a stalker or anything—he kind of looked like my father, tall, with faded red hair and dark brown eyes. "Can I help you with something? Were you looking for a palm reading?"

The man slid a look toward Ben before answering me. "Palm reading? No. Not unless . . . no. I am Lars Laufeyiarson. The young man taking care of the Andalusian gelding told me that the other horse belongs to you, is that correct?"

"Tesla? Yeah, I guess he belongs to me."

His forehead wrinkled. "You guess? You are not certain? Are you not his legal owner?"

"Yes, I'm certain. My mom made me get a receipt from the guy I bought Tesla from before we left Hungary. I'm his legal owner. Why do you want to know? Tesla hasn't been loose, so I know he couldn't have done anything, or gotten into any trouble—"

"I wish to purchase him," the man said abruptly, sliding Ben another wary look. "I will pay you one thousand dollars American for him."

CHAPTER THREE

I swear my jaw just about hit my feet when Mr. Laufeyiarson offered a grand for Tesla. A thousand dollars! For a horse! *My* horse? Something was definitely not right.

"You want to pay a thousand *dollars* for Tesla?" I asked, thinking maybe he was offering me a thousand of some other currency, something that sounded big, but really only meant ten bucks.

Mr. Laufeyiarson nodded. "Yes, one thousand dollars American."

Maybe he had the wrong horse? Maybe he thought Bruno was Tesla? Bruno had to be worth a ton of money; he knew all sorts of moves and special tricks, but Tesla? Tesla was just an old horse who like to snuffle people for treats, and occassionally allowed me to ride him around a field at a slow pace. "I don't want to sound insulting, Mr. Laufeyiarson, but are you sure you're talking about Tesla, and not Bruno? He's Andalusian, and very valuable—"

He shook his head. "No, the Andalusian is a gelding. I'm interested in the Lipizzan stallion."

I slid a confused glance toward Ben. He stood next to me, his arms crossed over his chest, watching me with dark oak eyes with pretty sparkly gold flecks. "Um . . . that's really nice of you, Mr. Laufeyiarson, but I don't think I could sell Tesla. I kind of promised a girl in Hungary that I'd take care of him."

"I understand. You have received another offer, yes? I will match the offer. How much do you want?" He pulled out a big leather wallet. My eyes bugged at the amount of money he had stuffed into it. "I brought fifteen hundred in cash, but if the offer was for more—"

"No!" I yelped, holding up a hand as he started digging out the wad of money. "There's been no other offer, honest. I just don't want to sell Tesla."

He frowned at me, a kind of puzzled look in his eyes that cleared as he looked at Ben. He said something in a language that wasn't English. Surprise flickered across Ben's face for a moment, and then he answered in the same language. A few seconds later, Mr. Laufeyiarson gave me a long, considering look, then inclined his head. "I see. I regret you could not accommodate me. If you change your mind, you may reach me at any time."

I looked down at the card he pushed into my hand before he walked off, leaving me to wonder just what was going on, what Ben had told him, and why he thought I would change my mind. Time for some answers.

"All right, what did all that mean?"

"All what?" Ben didn't wait for me to reply. He grabbed my hand and tugged me toward the area where the trailers were parked, stopping when we were hidden by shadows.

"All that he looked at you, and you looked at him, and you both did that secret guy talk thing that males do, and then Mr. Laufeyiarson left. Hey! You can't kiss me again!"

"I can't? Why not?" Ben pulled me into his arms and I stood for a moment, queen of indecision. Part of me— the girly part—wanted to swoon up against him and breathe in that wonderful Ben smell that was part leather jacket, part woodsy outdoors, but the other part of me—the brainy part—reminded the rest of me that he had disappeared for the past three weeks without any sort of an explanation, without even a good-bye.

"Because you already had your welcome back kiss, and now it's time to start explaining a few things, like where you've been, and why you went away without saying anything to me or Imogen, and who Mr. Laufeyiarson was, and why would anyone want to pay a thousand dollars for an old gray horse?"

"Tesla's a Lipizzan. I told you he was valuable," Ben said, ignoring the more important questions. At least he let go of me so I could step back and get a little distance from him. "Obviously this man recognized his blood-lines, and thinks stud rights are worth the money despite the stallion's age."

"You didn't say Tesla was valuable," I said, frowning. Stud rights? Someone wanted Tesla to get busy with a mare? My old creaky Tesla who had to walk around for a couple of hours to work out the stiffness in his joints? Valuable? "Do you think he was, like . . . oh, I don't know, stolen or something? Maybe I should write to my friend in Hungary and ask her how her grandfather got him."

Ben shrugged. "I meant to look into Tesla's past while I was in Hungary, but I was . . . er . . . sidetracked."

"By what?" I asked, my attention immediately yanked away from the mystery of Tesla.

Ben just looked at me. I made an annoyed sound and stripped off both gloves of my right hand, scratching an ichy spot on the back of it before placing my palm against the patch of skin exposed above the neckline of his black T-shirt. Ben was one of the few people who could close off his mind to me so I wasn't overwhelmed with all sorts of emotions. Now all I felt was a deep, burning red hunger.

I sighed and pulled my hand back. I didn't really want to, but I knew if I continued to stand there touching him, I'd end up kissing him again, and I really wanted some answers. A little spot on the side of my head tickled. I scratched it and said, "You know, you don't have to shut off all your emotions. A few would be helpful."

Even in the darkness of the shadows I could see his teeth flash white in a quick grin. "If you knew everything, then there would be no mystery to keep you coming back to me."

My nose itched. I scratched it as I answered. "Any more mystery and I'm going to start thinking a less annoying boyfriend is the way to go. So you were in Hungary after we left?"

My cheek itched. Ben said nothing as I scratched my cheek.

"What exactly were you doing in Hungary? Something to do with this job you have that you won't tell me anything about?"

The back of my neck almost twitched it itched so badly. I scratched it with both hands, mentally cursing the fact that Ben couldn't lie to me. Not that I wanted him to lie, but I'd found out that it was more annoying to have him refuse to speak than to try to decide whether what he was saying was true.

"And what happened to your cross? You're not wearing it anymore. You haven't suddenly gone all vampy about it, have you? You told me you could wear crosses and go into churches and all that stuff—has something changed?"

"No, nothing has changed," he said, his eyebrows pulling together as I reached behind me with both hands, yanked up the back of my shirt, and scratched like mad at a really itchy spot on my spine. "Have you picked up fleas from Tesla?"

"I don't have fleas!" I said, outraged, as I leaned against the trailer and rubbed my back on a protruding bit of metal. The itch wasn't appeased, but figured it couldn't hurt to try. "And neither does Tesla!"

"Then why are you hopping around like you are covered in itching powder?"

"It's my mother. It must be time for the circle to form. This is her subtle way of telling me she wants me."

His black eyebrows rose. "She torments you when she wants you?"

"It's just a simple itching spell," I said over my shoulder as I started toward the clearing beyond the Faire area where the circle was going to be held. "Nothing harmful, only really irritating until she stops it. You want to come to the circle?"

He shook his head. "Most witches don't care to have one born of the dark powers diluting their purity."

I debated telling him that Mom didn't think of him as evil just because he was a vampire, but seventeen different spots on me itched like mad, which meant my mother was upping the wattage in her spell. "Come on, no one will mind." I grabbed Ben's hand and hauled him after me as I jogged toward the flat area behind the main tent where my mother was holding her circle.

"Fran—" Ben dug in his heels and stopped.

"What? Oh, the sun! Sorry. Is it light enough to bother you?"

"Not so long as I remain covered," he answered, tugging his hat so it shaded his face.

"Good." I pulled on his hand. "Come on. Please? I missed you. I want to hear about what you've been doing, and tell you about all the interesting things I've been up to since we left Hungary."

He gave in, giving my hand a little squeeze before letting it go to wrap his arm around my waist. I went a little squidgy at that, but didn't have time to analyze just what that feeling meant—and what I should do about it—before we burst out into the circle.

"There you are," Mom started to say, stopping when she saw Ben with me. She held a sword in her hand, the sword she used to draw circles. The other ladies in the circle—there were five of them, including two members of GothFaire—gasped as a group, like they were shocked that Ben was there.

"I will leave," he said quietly.

I tightened my hold on his hand. "If you're not welcome, then I'm not staying."

"Fran . . ." Mom frowned for a moment, looking where I held Ben's hand hidden against my skirt so he wouldn't get sunburned, then to his face, thrown into shadow by the brim of his hat.

I don't want to make trouble, Fran. It's better if I leave.

You just got here! If you leave, I leave.

Mom sighed. "Very well, you may stay, Benedikt. But please do not interfere with the proceedings."

"We won't say a word," I promised, moving aside to stand with the others. Mom had evidently just completed drawing the first circle, the one cast in the sight of the gods. She did that by drawing a circle on the ground with the sword.

Have you ever been to a Wiccan circle? I asked Ben as he scooted over behind me. I turned so I'd block him from the weak sunlight peeking over the horizon.

No. Dark Ones are generally considered tainted. What is your mother doing?

Mom held a sword at waist level and walked the boundaries of the first circle she'd drawn.

A circle is drawn in three passes—the first is in honor of the gods. She did that before we got here. This one is to honor nature. The third signifies the spiritual level of the circle.

Ah. Mom walked the third circle with the sword held

31

over her head. *Interesting. I had imagined there would be some sort of invocation or words spoken.*

Oh, there will be, don't worry. She'll do the invocation to the god and goddess after she welcomes everyone into the circle. See? She's getting the annointing oil now. Sometimes she uses flowers to welcome people to the circle, or honey, or even incense, but it looks like tonight is going to be oily-forehead night.

Oily forehead?

Desdemona, GothFaire's time-travel counselor, stepped forward into the circle. Mom annoined her on the forehead with a drop of oil. Desdemona bowed her head as if she was honoring my mother, but I saw her sneaking a peek at Ben. I moved a smidgen closer to him, doing my best to convince myself that I wasn't jealous.

I like it best when she uses wine to welcome everyone to the circle, I said, smiling into Ben's mind. He smiled back as I followed Mikaela into the circle. A rich, pungent, spicy scent curled up as my mother touched my forehead and murmured a few words of what I knew was a blessing. I sniffed happily. She was using frankincense and myrrh oil, my favorite annointing oil. I took that as a sign that good things were going to happen, a thought that soured somewhat when I noticed Desdemona was still watching Ben.

Navy, a nice woman who was really, really preggers (she was the wife of Armand the demonologist), entered the circle next. She went to sit next to Mikaela and one of the local Wiccans. Mom hesitated a moment when Ben, the last person remaining, stepped into the circle. Everyone else held their breath for a moment, but once my mother decides to do something, she does it. She touched Ben on the forehead with the oil, saying the standard blessing.

Something within the circle changed at that moment, though, something I'd never felt before in a circle. It was like something had awakened from a long sleep. The pendant I wore beneath my shirt hummed to life, glowing with a warm heat.

Fran? What's wrong? Ben asked. I could feel his concern wrap around me like a soft velvet blanket.

Nothing, I said, trying to pinpoint what it was that felt different.

Something is bothering you. What is it?

I went to sit at the spot my mother indicated. Ben paused a minute when she pointed out to him a spot across the circle from me, but he went when I gave him a mental push. *Nothing. It's just this midnight sun thing, I think. It always throws me off. It's just weird being able to see everything in the middle of the night.*

You will tell me if you are unhappy about something, he said in his bossy voice.

I rolled my eyes at him. *I might have said I want to do the girlfriend thing with you, but that does not give you the right to push me around.*

Of course it does. You're my Beloved. It is my job to protect you from all evils.

OK, I admit—I went a bit girly at that. Not at his bossiness—that annoyed the crap out of me, and was something we had argued about a lot before we he disappeared and we came to Sweden—but at the fact that Ben really did want to keep me safe from things. I would have argued that fact now, but my mother pulled out handful of dried lavender branches, and started sweeping the circle.

This is a cleansing ritual, I told Ben as she moved along the circle, pausing to touch each person's feet with the lavender. *It's supposed to clean the circle of bad influences.*

Why is she touching our feet?

That's to clean you, too. It's all symbolic. Mom says a lot of witches use brooms for this, but she thinks that's way too stereotyped. She likes lavender instead.

"We will now begin the invocation to the god and goddess," my mother announced, having completed the cleansing. "Normally I would now call the quarters, but because our Asatru brothers and sisters are holding a *blot* a short distance away, we do not wish to disturb their forces by drawing their attention away. Thus, we will content ourselves with inviting the goddess and the god to join our circle."

Here comes the invocation part, I told Ben. *Inviting the goddess into the circle is called "drawing down the moon." Doing the same for the male god is called "drawing down the sun."*

Hmm. Two gods only?

Yup. Male and female halves, basically.

My mother stood in the center of the circle, her eyes closed, her arms spread out as she spoke the invocation to the goddess.

"Air, Water, Earth, Fire,
Elements of the stars conspire.
Goddess, mother of all, come to us!

Into the circle, right next to the bus."

I blinked in surprised. That wasn't the normal invocation. Evidently Mom realized something was wrong too because she opened her eyes and squinted at a nearby school bus that had been converted into a trailer for Desdemona. She shook her head, closed her eyes again, and centered herself.

"Keep us safe from curse or threat,

Just like a deodorant that guards from sweat."

Someone snickered. Mom had her eyes open again, frowning at nothing.

Er . . . that seems a rather incongruous invocation, Ben noted.

It's not right. Those aren't the correct words. For some reason, she's not saying it right, I answered. *Crapbeans. I wonder what's going on?*

I couldn't tell you.

"My apologies, sisters. Er, and brother," Mom said, shooting Ben a quick look. "I seem to be a bit . . . off tonight. I beg your indulgence."

"Of course, you have it," Desdemona said. She sat near me, which was good in one respect (I didn't like the way she kept shooting little glances at Ben), but for some reason, tonight her nearness made me feel edgy. I scooted a bit away from her, hoping no one would notice. Wiccans were very big on maintaining contact in a circle. To back away from someone was an insult.

Mom took a deep breath and gave it another shot.

"From sea and mountain, desert and trees,

By staff and sword and a mangy dog's fleas,

Heed our plea!"

Silence fell on the circle.

"Oh, dear," Navy said, leaning over to talk to one of the local Wiccans. "That's not right, is it?"

"Earth, Fire, Water, Air," Mom said grimly, her hands fisted as she started the invocation to the god.

"Elements of the stars conspire,
God, father of all, come to us!
Don't worry about being male, we'll make no fuss.
Guard us within from all threats beyond
I wonder if there are leeches in yonder pond?
By wand and cup and ball and bat
I just know these pants make my butt look fat.
Heed our plea!"

Desdemona burst out into laughter at the invocation. I wanted to giggle as well, but one look at the horror on my mother's face killed all thoughts of that. Clearly something was up to throw my mother so far off the track. I couldn't ask her what was wrong, though, because right at that moment, things got *really* weird.

"Goddess above—is that what I think it is?" Mikaela asked, pointing at me.

"Huh?" I asked, looking down at myself to see if I'd spilled something on me. Ben stood up, staring past me. I turned around to look and saw a thin, pretty woman with lots of long blond hair in the shadow of the tent behind me.

"It's a *huldra*," one of the local Wiccans said, her voice all hushed with awe. Or something.

"Is that a *tail?*" I asked as the stranger bent down to pick up something from the ground. I could have sworn there was a cow's tail popping out from under her long skirt.

"Yes, huldra have tails," Mikaela said, also getting to her feet. "They are spirits of the wood. A type of nymph, actually. They are supposedly harbingers of disaster, appearing briefly to warn of impending danger, then disappearing just as quickly—"

"Hey!" I yelled, jumping up as the woman snatched up the purse I'd set down in order to join the circle. "That's mine!"

"Franny, no! Do not break the circle—"

I knew it was bad to leave a circle before it had been formally unmade, but I couldn't just let the woman—spirit, nymph, whatever she was!—run off with my purse. It had all my money in it, for one thing, and for another, I just don't like people stealing from me. So I bolted after her as she raced past the main tent, heading straight for a small clump of scraggy trees that marked the boundary of the archealogical dig.

You should never run after a being you do not know, Ben chastised, his dark shape leaping past me after the blond huldra.

You're so cute, I thought at him, puffing just a little as I jumped over a fallen tree trunk. Ben was faster than me (he had longer legs plus that whole immortal thing going for him), but I wasn't going to just stand around and let him be Mr. Manly and get my purse back. Anyone who had to the nerve to steal from me had to deal with *me*, not my boyfriend.

The archealogical dig was at the far edge of the island.

It didn't look like much—a bunch of deep trenches and areas where square blocks of stone had been dug out and revealed, but evidently it was hot stuff archealogically speaking. Right in the center of the dig, in a ragged rectangular spot framed with bits of stone that Imogen had told me was the long house (the main living place of the Vikings who built this area), Tibolt and his gang were having their *blot*, also in a circle. Because the trees surrounding the area made it dark, they'd lit a few torches and stuck them in the ground, the light cast by them making odd little flickering shadows on everyone as they did whatever it is they did during a *blot*.

I stopped for a minute to survey the situation. Imogen was there, as I knew she would be, looking like a goddess in a shimmering gold-and-white dress as she stood next to Tibolt. He was dressed in some sort of long black robe, I guess his mage wear. I didn't pay too much attention to what was going on in the *blot* circle because beyond them, the huldra dashed out from behind a tree, and went racing across the dig site toward an unpassable rocky area.

Fran, let me catch her, Ben said as his shadow flickered in and out amongst the trees. He was following the path the huldra made, but I could tell he wasn't going to catch her before she got to the rock cliff. I sprinted to my right, along the outer edge of the *blot*, hoping to intercept her.

"Fran!" Tibolt yelled, startling me for a second. "No, you must not be here!"

"Don't worry, I know better than to intrude on a circle," I answered him, flinging myself forward to scramble onto a loose pile of earth that had been excavated from one of the nearby pits. The huldra was heading straight for me, too busy watching Ben over her shoulder to notice me about to tackle her.

"No, Fran, you must leave—"

Suddenly, the huldra whipped her head around just as I was getting ready to spring and veered to avoid my tackle. Instead, she jumped up onto the dirt mound with me, my purse clutched in one hand, the other outstretched like she was going to push me backward into the cleared area. The ground beneath my feet evidently objected to having two people on it, because it simply gave away beneath us, sending both the huldra and me falling backward into the excavation—and the *blot* circle.

My body broke the circle and I hit the ground hard, right at Imogen's feet. The huldra landed next to me. The impact had knocked the air out of both of us. A loud noise shook the ground like an earthquake. I ignored it as I threw myself on the huldra, yanking my purse from her hand. She snarled something at me in Swedish that I was willing to bet wasn't polite at all.

"Luspudlar!" I shot at her, the worst thing I'd learned to say so far (it meant lice-ridden poodle). I spat out a bit of earth, pushing my hair back from my eyes so I could add a glare that would teach her to mess with me. "No, son of a *luspudel* . . . holy bullfrogs!"

Around us, silence fell. Not a normal silence, the kind you get when a dozen or so people all decked out in robes and fringed dresses stand around the middle of the night sacrificing mead, but a heavy silence. A stunned silence. A silence that pretty much says, "Hey now! Something is seriously wrong here!"

Are you all right? Ben asked, sticking out a hand to pull me up.

Yeah. Or maybe not. Am I seeing what I think I'm seeing?

To the left, Tibolt sank to the ground, his head in his hands as he moaned something unintelligble.

That depends, Ben answered, his fingers tightening around mine. The huldra shrieked and ran off into the night. No one paid her any attention. *Are you talking about the* blot, *the fact that you scraped your wrist on a rock when you fell, or the Viking ghosts that just materialized around us?*

CHAPTER FOUR

"It is the valknut," Tibolt moaned as we all stood around, stunned. The *blot* people—about five of them—had broken the circular formation and were now huddled together in a group. Surrounding all of us were about a dozen men, all wearing basically nothing but leather and cloth leggings, each one carrying a really big sword. None had on a silly horned helmet (Mikaela told me later real Vikings didn't wear them), but I knew without anyone saying anything that we were looking at real Vikings—or rather, *dead* real Vikings. Viking ghosts, probably the guys who had died at this site.

To be honest, they looked as surprised to see us as we were to see them.

"I told you it had the power to raise the dead. That is why I gave it to you to wear tonight—to keep it from the power of the *blot*."

"Oh, the pendant?" I pulled it out of my shirt, absently noticing that it felt three times heavier than normal. "You said it had something to do with the Fates, not that it was going to do a Viking zombie sort of thing."

The nearest Viking strolled over and peered at the pendant. Ben moved to stand next to me, a protective gesture that simultaneously warmed my heart and annoyed me. "Ah. *Vikingahärta*," the Viking said, nodding, then turned to his fellow ghosts and yelled something that had them all screaming like banshees.

"What the heck is that?" I asked, scooching closer to Ben. He wrapped an arm around my waist. I didn't protest at all, not with a dozen screaming Viking ghosts standing around.

"I think it's their war cry," Ben answered.

"They are happy to be resurrected," Tibolt said, finally looking up. "They are calling to Tyr, the god of war. It's all over now."

"All over? What is all over?" Imogen asked, looking worried. "I don't understand what has happened here. Why are there ghosts? What has Fran's necklace to do with it? And why are they shouting *'holle, holle'* at her?"

I was about to ask that last question myself. The Viking who had checked out the valknut was back in front of me, raising his sword in the air as he lead a chant.

"Holle was the goddess of the dead," Tibolt said, getting to his feet. His shoulders sagged, like he was tired, and for the first time since I'd met him, he didn't seem to hold the same attraction for me. I wondered if his glamor, or whatever it is he'd been using had worn off, or if the pendant had something to do with it. "She is the daughter of Loki. The valknut, combined with the power invoked by the *blot* is what raised them. What has happened here is unfortunate—I had hoped to avoid this outcome, since he is near. But what's done is done."

"Um . . . where are you going?" I asked as he gathered up a small leather bag and started to walk away. The other *blot*ters did likewise, although they also shot confused little looks between Tibolt and the Vikings. "Are you going to get something to put these ghosts back?"

"No," he answered without even turning his head. "I do not have the means to do that."

"Who does?" Ben called out after him. Imogen moved over to stand next to us, eyeing the Vikings as if they were aliens.

"The master," Tibolt said, then he and the blotters disappeared into the woods, leaving the three of us surrounded by Viking ghosts.

"Master? What master?" Imogen asked, frowning slightly.

"Anyone who calls himself the master can't be good," Ben said, eyeing the ghosts. "But that's a moot point since he's not here, and we are. I suppose we should leave as well."

"And do what?" I asked, waving my hand toward them. "Just leave them here yelling and stuff? Ben, they're ghosts! The dig crew is going to get here in the morning and find ghosts wandering around their site. You think no one is going to notice that?"

He sighed, his mind a soft touch against mine. *It is none of our concern.*

Yes, it is. I'm evidently the one who brought them back.

43

"It was not intentional," he argued, pulling me after him as he started to leave the dig site.

"That doesn't matter, I still—"

"You are leaving, Holle?" a voice asked from behind us. We spun around staring at the big Viking who had been next to me. "We just arrived. Why are you leaving us?"

"You speak English?" I asked, stunned, my feet coming to a halt.

"Of course. We have not much else to do over the centuries but watch the visitors and learn their languages." The Viking frowned. "I am Eirik Redblood. These are my men, my family, my brothers. Who do you wish for us to slaughter?"

"Slaughter?" I asked, the word coming out like a squeak. "No one!"

"Begone, spirit," Ben said, waving his hand toward Eirik. "We have no need of you in this place."

The Vikings all burst into laughter, a couple of them doubling over and wiping their eyes. Ben's eyebrows pulled together in a puzzled frown as he watched them. He lifted his hand toward them again, making the same waving gesture. "I command you to leave now."

That made the Vikings laugh even harder.

"Uh-oh," I said, peeking at Ben from the corner of my eye. He didn't look happy. *Was that little hand thingie supposed to do something?*

Yes.

Oops.

Eirik stalked over toward us, lifting his sword so the tip was almost touching Ben's throat. "You have no powers over us, Dark One. Not here, in the land that is soaked with our blood."

"OK. Time for us to leave, I think," I said, stepping backward carefully, tugging at the back of Ben's jacket. He didn't move, of course. "Um, Ben? Let's go."

"I will stay here until you and Imogen are safely away," he answered in his macho guy voice. I almost rolled my eyes, but didn't because there is a time and place for eye rolling, and doing it while a big, bad Viking ghost holds a sword to your boyfriend's neck isn't one of them.

Eirik's blue eyes eyes narrowed as he looked at me. "You know this Dark One, Holle?"

"My name isn't Holly, it's Fran, and yes, I know him. He's . . . er . . . he's my . . ."

His eyes narrowed further. "Does he hold you prisoner?"

"Stay back, Fran," Ben said, moving slightly to the side to block Eirik's view of me.

"No," I said on a sigh, answering both Ben and Eirik's question with one word as I let go of Ben's jacket and stood beside him. "No, he doesn't hold me prisoner, and no, I'm not going to stay back. Ben is my boyfriend, OK? Now please move your sword. It's making me really nervous."

To my surprise, Eirik did as I asked. "By your will, Holle. Who would you have us destroy, if not this Dark One? The female?"

Imogen, who had been watching everything silently, gasped, her silver eyes flashing at him. "I would like to see you try!"

"Why do you keep asking me who I want destroyed?" I asked. "And why do insist on calling me Holle? I'm not the goddess of death, or whoever Tibolt said she was. My name is Fran, I work for the GothFaire, and Ben and Imogen are my friends."

"You raised us, so we are yours to command, oh mighty goddess Fran," Eirik said, dropping to one knee. "We are bound to you until you call the Valkyries to take us to Valhalla."

"Just when I thought my life couldn't get any weirder," I muttered.

"Other than the rude one who offered to kill me, I think they're rather charming," Imogen said, smiling at a half-naked Viking ghost. To my surprise, he smiled back at her.

Any ideas on what I should do to get rid of them? I asked Ben.

None, I'm afraid, he answered with a puzzled look on his face. *Ghosts are out of my range of experience. Most likely the best thing to do is ask them.* "How does Fran release you?" he asked Eirik.

Eirik's nostrils flared as he looked Ben over from head to toe. Ben wasn't as big and bulky as Eirik, but he wasn't a skinny little nothing, either. Beside me, all his muscles tensed like he was going to fling himself forward.

"You are mated to the goddess?" the Viking asked.

"Yes," Ben said without even a second's delay.

"Whoa! We are not mated!" I said, giving him a glare. "All I've done is kiss you!"

Eirik's eyes lit up as he took a step forward. "You are

not mated to the Dark One? Good. I have always desired to rut with a goddess."

"Rut?" I asked, holding my ground even though Eirik took another step toward me, because I didn't let anyone intimidate me. Ben's arm tightened around my waist.

"Swive," Eirik said, with a smile that made it pretty darn clear just what he was talking about.

"Oh, *that* mated! Silly me! Yes, yes we are. Ben and I, that is. We're *so* mated, like every night. Sometimes four or five times a night," I said, figuring more was better where that sort of thing was concerned. Ben I knew I could trust—with Eirik I wasn't really so sure.

"I'm not mated to anyone," Imogen said, smiling again at the Viking behind Eirik.

"Imogen!" Ben growled. "Behave yourself. They are ghosts."

"Yes, but such cute ones. Are you corporeal?" She walked forward and put her hand out toward the hottie Viking's chest. To my surprise, her hand didn't go whipping through him. Instead it stopped and rested on his bare chest. Imogen gave a little squeal of delight. "You are! How exciting!"

Ben swore under his breath. I pinched his hand to remind him that Imogen was not going to be happy if he made a fuss about whom she dated. "You didn't answer my question, Viking. How does Fran release you?"

Eirik looked at me. "I will answer him because he is mated to you, but if you change your mind about him at any time, I will be happy to—"

"Thanks," I said quickly, figuring we were all going to be happier if he didn't finish that sentence. "About the releasing thing?"

He shrugged. "You are a goddess, you must know best how to do that."

"But I'm not a goddess," I protested.

"You bear the *Vikingahärta*, and you called us to rise. Only a goddess could do such a thing," he insisted.

Great. Now what do I do? I'm so not a goddess.

"You don't know how she can release you?" Ben asked as I gave a mental groan.

"No," Eirik answered, looking slightly bored. "We are warriors, Vikings, children of the gods—not the gods themselves. Such things are no concern of ours."

Clearly the answer lies in the pendant, Ben said. *The blond man said earlier that it was responsible for raising the ghosts—perhaps if we knew more about it, we could discover how to use it to release the ghosts.*

Good idea. I'll ask Tibolt.

"What *are* your concerns?" Imogen asked, her voice silky as she stroked the Viking's chest.

"War!" Eirik shouted.

"Pillage!" another one answered.

"Women," the ghost Imogen was touching said in a near purr. They smiled again at each other.

"Oh, for Christ's sake—" Ben muttered to himself.

Would you like me to touch your chest like that? I asked him, watching Imogen as she murmured in the Viking's ear. He laughed and leaned down to whisper in her ear as well.

Ben's eyes, normally a delicious brown with gold and

black flecks in them, went the color of honey oak. *Sweetheart, that would lead to us really being mated, which would mean we were Joined. And I don't think you're ready for that yet.*

Gotcha. No chest touchies.

A little sigh of unhappiness swept through him, but he cut it off before I could say anything. "Let's go find this Tibolt."

"OK," I said, turning toward the camp, but Ben didn't follow me like I expected. Instead he and Eirik were toe-to-toe. "What now?"

"He was going with you," Ben growled, doing the macho bit I was starting to think he really loved. I sighed to myself. That was one of the things we had yet to work out, but I figured right then was not the time to do it.

"You guys don't want to stay here?" I asked Eirik, waving my hand to indicate the dig site. "You said this was your home, right?"

"Until you summoned us. Now we follow you," Eirik answered, and sure enough, they all got in line behind him, Imogen's Viking giving her a steamy look as he did so.

"You are not going to annoy Fran in any way," Ben said stubbornly, crossing his arms over his chest.

I walked back to him and put a hand on his arm, giving his biceps a little squeeze (which, I had to admit, made me do a little inner girly squeal, but he didn't need to know that). "Remember rule number one—Fran can take care of herself. Good. So you can stop being all manly and stuff and let *me* worry about me."

Ben shot me an outraged look that pretty much told me what he thought of rule number one.

"Hey, Imogen and I beat up a demon last month all by ourselves!" I stopped squeezing and whapped him on the arm. "We stopped him from killing you, too!"

"I had the situation fully in my control," he answered, his voice low like he was growling. For some reason, that just made me want to kiss him. "If you and Imogen hadn't interefered—"

"Oh, for heaven's sake, little brother," Imogen said as she strolled over to us. "This is 2006, not 1806. Fran and I are quite capable of taking care of not only ourselves, but you, as well."

"I don't need anyone to take care of me," Ben sputtered, his eyes going black as he glared at his sister.

Imogen smiled at him and kissed his cheek. He growled some more. "So typical of Moravian men. I've done my best with him, Fran, but clearly you have a lot of work ahead of you. I believe I shall drive over to the mainland and see what's happening at the local nightclub." She cast a glance over her shoulder at her friendly Viking. "If anyone would care to join me, I'd be happy to have the company."

Ben opened his mouth like he was going to forbid her, but I dug my nails into his wrist, so he just glared at me instead.

Imogen's Viking looked first at Eirik, then at me. I realized with a bit of surprise that he was waiting for permission. "Sure," I said, waving at Imogen. "Knock yourself out. All of you. I . . . er . . . hereby do solemnly give you permission to do whatever you want to do without asking me first. Unless it's like something bad, then don't do it. OK?"

The Vikings scattered like pool balls, a couple of them going off with Imogen to the nearest town on the mainland, a couple heading for the main tent, the rest off to wander around the fairgrounds. Only Eirik remained standing with Ben and me.

"Don't you want to go to town with Imogen and the others?" I asked, kind of surprised that he'd want to stay behind.

"No. My duty is to stay near my goddess in case she has need of me," he said, falling into place on my left side as Ben walked on my right. We were headed toward the lights and noise of the Faire, which still had a few hours to go.

"I will take care of any needs Fran has," Ben said stiffly.

We are so going to have a little talk later, I told him.

Yes. Yes, we are. It's about time we have a few things out.

I sent him a mental frown, and decided he needed to be ignored for a minute or two. "So, you guys all died together here?" I asked Eirik. "Was it . . . um . . . bad? Dying?"

"We fought and died with much honor," he said proudly. "There were twelve of us to the Norwegians' ten score. We sent three times our number to Valhalla before they finished us."

"Wow. That's a lot of killing."

"We are Viking. It's what we do best," he said modestly. "There is a priestess in your group, is there not? I have seen her. She has hair the color of a crow, which stands up in unruly clumps. If I cannot rut with a goddess, a priestess would do."

51

"That would be Mikaela, but she has a husband," I said, sliding a quick glance toward Ben. "There's a girl working for the Faire who doesn't have a boyfriend, though. Her name is Desdemona. She's a personal time-travel counselor."

"Hmm." Eirik looked thoughtful.

"Fran? Where did you—oh. Hi, Benedikt. Who's that?" We'd reached the edge of the fairgrounds, keeping to the shadows as much as possible because of Ben. Soren popped out of the main tent and stood with his hands on his hips, squinting first at Ben, then at Eirik. "Why is he dressed so funny?"

"He's a ghost, and a Viking, and I'm sure it's not funny to him," I said, making warning eyebrows at Soren. "Eirik, this is Soren. He's the son of the one of the owners of the Faire, and is a magician in training. He's also teaching me to ride. Soren, this is Eirik Redblood, leader of the Vikings who were killed over at the dig site. He's . . . uh . . . been called back accidentally."

Soren blinked twice, then nodded. "A Viking ghost. OK. How long will he be here?"

"Er . . . we're not quite sure on that. There are eleven others, as well, although some went off with Imogen to the local disco." I wrinkled my nose as something occurred to me. "What are people in town going to think of a bunch of guys dressed in leather and leggings?" I asked Ben.

He shrugged one shoulder. "It could start a new fashion trend."

"Where is this Desdemona you speak of?" Eirik asked me, scanning the crowds wandering around the fairgrounds. Even though he stood a good head higher than everyone else, and was dressed like ye olde Viking, no one seemed to be paying him any attention. Everyone milled around the various booths and stalls that formed an alley, slowly drifting past us into the main tent, where the second round of magic acts were about to start.

I pointed down to the far end of the right side of booths. "See the big hourglass above the green-striped awning? That's Desdemona's booth. The second show is about to start, so most people will go watch that if you wanted to talk to her. Although I should warn you— she's a bit wacky when it comes to the subject of time travel."

Soren snickered. "You just say that because she insists you're the reincarnation of Cleopatra."

Ben laughed, taking my hand and rubbing his thumb over the ring I wore, a ring that had once belonged to his mother, but which he'd given me last month. "Fran?"

"Hey, you don't have to say that in such a disbelieving tone," I said. "I could be Cleopatra!"

"I don't believe in reincarnation," he said, smiling at me.

"I don't know what this time travel is, but I like to sail. I will try it," Eirik said, and without another word he went marching off down the row toward Desdemona's booth.

"He's in for a surprise," I said, smiling.

"Ja. Big surprise." Soren looked up as his father and my mother walked over to us.

I flinched. Mom had a really unhappy look on her face, but all she said was, "I will speak to you later about your behavior in the circle."

"Soren, is Bruno ready?" Peter asked, cocking an eyebrow at his son. "No? Then go, the show is about to begin. Ah. Ben, you are back with us?"

"I am," Ben said, shaking Peter's hand. "I will probably be around for a while. I'm staying with Imogen, so if there is something I can do to help out, let me know."

"I will, thank you." Peter yelled something at one of the guys hauling in a crate containing his illusion equipment. "I must go now. I have told them a hundred times how valuable that equipment is, but they do not listen—"

Peter hurried off to set up the second show. Mom gave me a warning look and drifted off. Ben rubbed his chin as he looked after her. "I wonder what was going on with her invocations."

"Probably that huldra. Or the ghosts. Her invocations can go wonky if there are unsettled elements in the area." I shrugged and smiled. "So, you're going to be here for a while this time? No running off without a word to anyone?"

His thumb rubbed over my knuckles. My knees went a bit weak at the touch, but I told them to knock off the girly stuff. "I'm sorry about that. It was unavoidable, but I regret not being able to tell you I had to leave before I was called away."

"Called away by who?" I asked, throwing grammar rules to the wind.

He just rubbed my fingers and didn't answer. I sighed. Just because he couldn't lie to me, didn't mean he had to keep silent whenever I asked a question he didn't want to answer. I mean really.

"I'm not going to tell anyone if you've been off doing something, you know"—I made bitey claw fingers—"vampy. You can trust me, Ben. I'm not going to give you away."

"I trust you with my life," he said, pulling my hand up to give my fingers a kiss. My stomach did a happy back-flip. "But this situation concerns someone other than me, and I am not at liberty yet to tell you about it."

I sighed again. "OK. Mom says I have to respect your privacy, although she did say a couple of snarky things about guys who run off without a word. But I trust you, too, so I'm not going to say anything more about it. For now."

He smiled and kissed my fingers again, his breath warm on my suddenly sensitive knuckles. Who knew a hand could be so sexy?

"But . . . um . . . that brings up another subject." I bit my lip, a little embarassed. I reminded myself that there was nothing wrong with it, and blurted it out quickly, before I changed my mind. "I know that a guy normally asks this, but I'm into equal rights and stuff, so I was wondering if you'd like to go on a date with me? A real date, not a ride on your bike like we did in Hungary, but a real date date, the kind where I dress up and stuff. Maybe we could get some dinner and see a movie or something, if they have English movies here. Or what-ever. If you don't want to, that's fine, too. I just thought maybe—"

He laughed and gave me a quick kiss, almost a non-kiss, just a brush of his lips. It was enough to stop me from blathering on and on, but not enough to make anyone notice us. "I would love to go on a date. Dinner and a movie sounds great. When would you like to go?"

It took me a few seconds to get over the kiss. "How about on Sunday? There's just one show on Sunday nights, and we can go after the last magic act."

"Three days from now?" he asked, smiling.

"Yeah, well, I'm kind of booked until then," I said, trying to sound sophisticated. What I didn't tell him is that my stomach was turning somersaults at the idea of a real, honest-to-goddess date with him. I'd need those three days just to get myself to the point where I could go out with him without spending the entire time kissing him. Which is what I wanted to do now. Just standing near him made me feel tingly, kind of the same way the pendant felt.

"Very well, Sunday it is." He stepped back behind the demonology booth, pulling me into the shadow with him. "Perhaps we should seal the deal with a kiss?"

"Sounds good to me," I said, leaning up against him, drinking in the wonderful leather/spicey smell that was pure Ben.

"Let's hear the name of that Welsh place again," he said, his eyes going almost golden.

I was just about to say it when Soren ran out into the main aisle, yelling my name. Soren doesn't run well because of his leg, so for him to be moving that fast had to mean something was up. "I'm right here—what's going on?" I asked as Ben and I stepped into the aisle.

"It's Tesla," Soren said, limping toward me, a lead rope in his hand.

"Oh, no, is something wrong with him? Is he sick?" I

asked, starting toward the area where the horses were kept.

"I don't know," Soren yelled after me as Ben and I ran toward the pasture. "He's not there. He's gone. I think he's been stolen."

CHAPTER FIVE

Soren was right. I had my doubts when he said he thought Tesla had been stolen—who'd want an old dirty white horse? But the area where Tesla and Bruno had been hobbled was empty. Tesla's hobble was sitting neatly on a rock, right next to the water bucket.

"Someone took this off," Ben said, fingering the open buckles. "It didn't come off on its own."

"Do you see?" Soren asked as he puffed his way up to us. "He was taken, *ja?*"

"Looks that way." I hesitated a minute, then stripped off the layers of latex and lace gloves I wore to keep from reading everything I touched, and held out my hand for the hobble. Ben placed it across my palm, careful to keep from touching my hand. Although he was one of the few people I didn't mind touching, I didn't want to confuse my psychometry abilities by picking up on something he was feeling rather than the person who unbuckled the hobble.

"Well?" Soren asked as I sorted through the images

that came to mind as soon as my fingers closed over the leather cuff. "Who took him? Is Bruno in danger? I should tell my dad if there is a horse kidnapper around."

"I don't think this is a horsenapper," I said, focusing on hobble.

"Who touched it, Fran?" Ben asked, his voice quiet but full of concern. He knew how much Tesla meant to me.

"Ben, Soren, Peter, Karl . . ." Those last three made sense. They all helped take care of the horses, loading and unloading them in the horse trailer when we move to another town, so it was no surprise that at one time or another they'd picked up the hobble. But it was a fifth person who'd touched it that worried me. ". . . and someone else. Someone I don't know. Someone . . . *different*."

"Different how?" Ben asked. I handed him back the hobble and turned to scan the open field. I didn't think Tesla would be hidden away in the shadows, but I had to look anyway.

"Different as in not human."

"What?" Soren asked, his mouth hanging open. "Not human? You mean like a ghost?"

"I don't know what he is, other than he doesn't have any feeling whatsoever."

"No feelings?" Soren frowned.

"Yeah. None whatsoever. Everyone leaves some sort of residual emotion behind when they touch something, even Ben does when he tries to close off his emotions—I can feel that it's him that touched it. But the guy who touched the hobble wasn't normal. Not human."

"Or heavily shielded," Ben said, looking thoughtful.

"There are people who are able to block themselves completely. Mages and the like."

"Mages?" I looked down at the hobble. "Mikaela said Tibolt was a mage."

"You'd know if it was him who took Tesla, though," Soren pointed out, slapping at a mosquito on his arm.

I shook my head. "I haven't touched him with my bare hands." Something occurred to me then. "Oh great. I haven't touched a bunch of people working here—that means I'm going to have to go around doing the touchy-feely thing with everyone. I hate that!"

"That may not be necessary," Ben said, an odd abstracted look on his face. "There's a Diviner here, isn't there?"

"Diviner? Not that I know of."

"Hmm. Perhaps there's one nearby we can ask for help."

"Whatever," I said, anxious to find Tesla. "All this standing around talking isn't finding him. He could be out there all alone, or being abused or something. Ben? Can we go find him, please?"

"Absolutely. I'll get my bike and pick you up." He tossed the hobble next to the bucket and ran off to get his motorcycle.

"I'd help look, too, but the show is about to start," Soren said, casting a worried look over his shoulder toward the main tent. "In fact—"

"Go," I said, making shooing motions with both hands. "Don't be late with Bruno or your dad will kill you."

He hurried off, leaving me standing alone in the empty

field. I tried to open myself up to it. Mom said it was the proper way to get in touch with other beings and weird things like that, but I guess I lack the "opening up" gene or something, because all I felt was the night breeze and a couple of residual itchy spots.

"Ready?" Ben asked. I gave up and ran over to the field where people parked. He was on his bike, fiddling with one of the levers (it had to be a guy thing—I didn't hear anything wrong with the bike at all), his long black hair pulled back into a ponytail.

"I'm ready, although I don't know where to start looking. I guess we're going to have to check out everywhere we can— Ugh. Not that!"

I made a face at the helmet Ben held in his hand.

"It's your mother's rule," he said, giving it to me. I glared at it. I hated wearing a helmet, but my mother had put her foot down after she'd caught me riding around with Ben without one.

"You're not wearing one," I pointed out, knowing it was stupid to pout, but feeling like it anyway.

"That's because I'm immortal." He zipped up his leather jacket and held out his hand for me. "If we crash and I smash my head in, it won't do anything but make me pissed for a while. You're a bit more fragile."

"Well, you keep telling me I'm your Beloved and all. I thought they were immortal like Imogen?"

"Beloveds are immortal like female Moravians, yes, but you're not my Beloved yet. At least, not officially. Unless you want to do the blood exchange?"

I thought for a moment he was seriously pressing me to do the whole "save his soul by binding myself to him forever" thing, but his dark eyes were twinkling from under the shadow thrown by the brim of his hat.

"Another time, vamp boy," I said, giving him a little punch on the arm just to let him know I cared. He laughed and scooted forward a bit as I crawled onto the seat behind him, thankful I'd worn shorts instead of a skirt.

He glanced back at my bare knees, moving back until I was pressed up tight against his back. "I hope you won't be too cold."

"I figured you'd keep me warm." I leaned into his back, wrapping my arms around him as he gunned the bike and pushed off. It took me a few minutes to get my mind off the really delicious scent of leather jacket and Ben (he had to be wearing some sort of spicy aftershave or something), but eventually, I stopped snuffling his neck and ponytail, and started looking around as he drove us through the countryside.

We searched for Tesla until two in the morning. Because of the white night, we could zoom around and look for a horse being horsenapped pretty easily, but unfortunately, whoever took Tesla hid him well. By the time we got back to the fair, I was upset, mad, and frustrated.

"I'm sorry, Fran," Ben said as I climbed off his bike. I felt like crying, but I knew that was stupid—Tesla hadn't been hurt (at least I didn't think he had), he was just stolen. "I'll keep looking for him."

"Look where? We looked everywhere within a two-hour radius. If someone had driven off right away with him and kept driving, we'd never be able to find him anyway."

Ben got off the bike and pulled me into a hug. "We'll

find him, Fran. I promise you that we'll find him," he said, his breath ruffling my hair.

I leaned against him, an odd sense of rightness creeping over me that distracted me for a minute from Tesla. I had told Ben the previous month that I was willing for us to try the girlfriend/boyfriend thing, but I had said that just because I liked him so much. I didn't honestly buy into that whole Beloved bit—although it gave me a warm feeling to think about it—but right after we'd left Hungary for France, Ben disappeared to do whatever the mysterious thing was that he couldn't tell me, so we really hadn't had much time to be together.

And now there I was standing in his arms, leaning against him, feeling warm and happy despite the fact that I was worried sick about Tesla. I couldn't help thinking things were pretty wonderful because we were together, and also, I'm ashamed to say, I was more than a little smug because out of the millions of girls wandering around the world, Ben had picked *me*.

Life is kinda weird that way.

"Fran, are you ready for your regression? Oh, hello, Ben. We haven't been properly introduced, have we? Imogen has told me so much about you, though, I feel like I know you. I'm Desdemona. I'm a personal time-travel consultant. Did you know that in a past life Fran was Cleopatra? It's so very exciting. I've promised to regress her again so we can get some more fascinating details of her life in ancient Egypt."

Life just got a whole lot weirder.

Ben unwrapped his arms from around me as soon as Desdemona started to talk, but he didn't move away as I

63

turned around to face her. Part of me was embarassed that anyone had caught us together, but the other part was annoyed because it was clear the way Desdemona was smiling at Ben that she had purposely interrupted us.

"Hi, Des. About the regression—could we do it another time? I'm a bit busy right now."

"Yeeees," she drawled, giving Ben another long look. Her tone made me grit my teeth. And it didn't help that she was wearing a leather waist cincher and short skirt that let everyone see just how different her five-foot-nothing, one hundred-pound self was from mammoth, six-foot-tall me. "I can see you were."

"No, not us. Um. That is, Ben and I weren't . . . well, we were, but that's not what I'm talking about."

"Fran is distraught over the theft of her horse," Ben said smoothly interrupting me. *Are you by any chance jealous?*

Me? You're kidding right? I'm so not jealous. Although she definitely has the hots for you, the wench.

Ben laughed in my head.

"Oh, your horse was stolen? I'm so sorry. Of course the regression can wait for another time." Desdemona smiled at Ben. "How would you like a personal time-travel experience, Ben? It seems I have an opening, and since the fair is just now closing, I could get you in quickly."

Oh! She didn't just say that!

Calm down, Fran. She's harmless. "Another time, perhaps. I've promised Fran to continue looking for her horse, and I doubt if I'll be done before daybreak." Ben glanced toward where the sun was barely beneath the horizon. "Or as close to daybreak as it gets around here. Thank you anyway."

"No problem. I'll be happy to do you anytime," she said, giving us both a little wave as she strolled off toward the main tent. Ben watched her walk away from us for a second before looking back at me.

"Why are you making that face?" he asked. "Why are your eyes narrow little slits of ebony that look like they want to shoot lasers at me?"

"You watched her walk away," I said, struggling to keep my voice jealous-free. I lost the fight. "You deliberately watched."

"Yes, I did. I looked at her breasts, too, but despite that, you're still the only girl on the planet for me."

"Nice try, Vlad," I said, slipping out of his arms when he tried to pull me into another kiss. I stalked toward the trailer that Mom and I shared. "*My* boyfriend isn't going to be aware there's anyone else around but me. Since you have other ideas, so long. Hasta la vista. Don't let the door hit you on the butt going out."

Ben stood where I left him, his arms crossed over his chest. I smiled to myself where he couldn't see it.

Fran?

Hmm?

Are you seriously jealous of Desdemona, or are you ragging me a little?

What do you think?

I smiled even more at the pause that followed that. He wasn't one hundred percent sure, something I was perfectly happy about. I entered the trailer, absently moving Davide from the couch that turned into my bed at nights.

I think you know full well how much you mean to me. I think you know that I'd do anything to make you happy.

I think you know I can't exist without you, that you are heaven and earth to me, my salvation, my joy, my life.

This time I let him feel my smile.

The brush of his mind against mind had a decidedly disgruntled tone to it. *And I think you're enjoying every minute of keeping me on tenterhooks about whether or not you're going to be my Beloved.*

Goodnight, Ben, I said, laughing into his head. *Thank you for looking for Tesla.*

Sleep well, sweet Fran, he answered, and I give in and had a lovely sigh of happiness over him.

Even with the Tesla problem, life was looking pretty good at the moment. Ben was back, and as yummy as ever. I had settled into life with the GothFaire, and actually enjoyed doing the palm readings. Mom was happy with her new group of friends, the Faire was doing well, and even Soren was happy these days.

"Things are looking up for a change," I told Davide as I flipped off all the lights but one so Mom could see her way past me when she finished for the night, and settled into my makeshift bed. The big cat sauntered over, jumping up on me so he could sleep on my hip. It was his favorite spot, despite the fact that we didn't really like each other. "Not even poor Tesla gone missing, and half-naked Viking ghosts running around are going to ruin my date with Ben day after tomorrow. That is going to be the most perfect event of my life, I just know it."

Which just goes to show you I'm *not* clairvoyant in any way.

CHAPTER SIX

The first inkling I had that something was wrong the next morning was the war axe imbedded in the wooden door of my closet.

"Hrung?" I asked in no known language as I squinted at the wood and steel weapon that still vibrated slightly. The blade of the ax, mostly buried in the door, was curved on the edges. "Wha'?"

"Goddess, have you seen—oh, there it is." The Viking Imogen had been flirting with the night before stood at the open window right next to me. I glared at him, pulling the thin blanket covering my legs up over the jumbo T-shirt I wore to bed. "Would you mind giving me back my Hanwei ax?"

"You threw an ax at me?" I asked, my brain still sleepy and thus not much able to make sense of what he was saying.

"Me?" the Viking asked, pointing at himself in disbelief. "I would never do that! You are a goddess, and I am

67

merely Finnvid, your devoted servant and the slayer of many hundred Huns."

"Then what is that doing in here?" I pointed to the ax. He looked a bit abashed.

"It . . . er . . . slipped. I was aiming at an usurper, and it went through your window rather than cleaving his brain in two, as it was meant to do."

It was at that point I realized the sounds that had vaguely registered on my brain weren't from someone's portable TV or radio. I distinctly recognized Absinthe's brusque German voice as she yelled orders.

"What the bullfrogs—" A woman's loud scream from nearby had me jumping out of bed and racing to the door. Davide and my mother were gone, which meant they had probably already left to do their morning rituals to the god and goddess with their Wiccan friends. Since closing time wasn't until two in the morning, most of the GothFaire and Circus of the Darned people didn't get up until after noon, but there were a few hardy folk up earlier. I figured it was about nine in the morning as I flung open the door to the trailer. "Holy crap!"

The sight that met my eyes was not one I ever expected to see—only a handful of GothFairians were up, but they were active . . . very active. Running around screaming with various Vikings chasing after them.

"Is it?" The Viking ghost named Finnvid, who still stood by the open window, looked around, finally spotting a nearby pile of dog poop (probably made by Tallulah's pug, Wennie). "Ah. It looks like dog shite to me, but if it's holy, I will not rub someone's face in it."

The Faire was usually set up in the shape of a large U,

with the big tent at the bottom, and two arms of vendor tents and booths. To the far side of one of the arms was what Mom called Trailer Town—where Faire and Darned people set up their trailers and RVs. In the center of the vaguely circular arrangement of trailers were a couple of portable picnic tables and chairs, a small barbecue, and three folding chaise lounges that everyone used to work on their tans. The chaises weren't being used for suntanning now—one of them was acting as a trampoline for a red-haired Viking. while another was tipped up on its end, the elasticy plastic webbing being used by another Viking to catapult overly ripe peaches at Tallulah. She had taken refuge behind a plastic picnic table, but every time she popped her head up to see if the coast was clear, the Viking launched another peach at her. The trailer behind her was a slimy mess of gooey, dripping peach blobs that slumped their way to the ground. Peter would be furious. He had bought the peaches to feed his fruit addiction, and now they were smeared everywhere.

"What in the name of all that is good and glorious is going on here?" Mikaela emerged from the trailer next to ours, wearing a pair of jeans and a tank top. She held a bottle of water in one hand, and a candle and couple pieces of lavendar in the other.

"Brutta!" Finnvid shouted, and leaped past me to scoop her up.

Mikaela screamed and yelled for Ramon, her husband, while simultaneously beating Finnvid on the head with her water bottle. Beyond her, Absinthe had somehow made it to the top of her trailer, where she stood yelling what were no doubt rude things in German down to the three Vikings trying to scale the trailer to get to her.

Ramon burst out of his trailer with one leg in his pants, hopping on one foot while he tried to get the other leg in, at the same time dodging peaches from the Viking at the catapult.

"Fran!" Absinthe shrieked, jumping up and down on the trailer as she pointed at me. "These ghosts are yours! Control them!"

"They're not mine—"I yelled back, pausing for a minute as Peter emerged from between trailers. He walked backwards, a two-by-four in his hands to parry blows from a long, heavy sword. The owner of the sword lunged toward him, sending Peter falling over a lawn chair. While the peach-throwing Viking's attention was focused on Ramon, Tallulah ran to her trailer. But she stopped in the doorway and sent me a look that raised goose bumps on my arms. Although her lips didn't move, I swear I could hear her voice on the wind saying, "This is your doing. Fix it!"

"Hey!" I bellowed, and threw myself off the trailer steps when I saw that the person about to gut Peter was Eirik. "Stop that! I said no killing!"

Eirik paused in the act of beheading Peter. "No, you didn't. You said you didn't have anyone you wanted us to kill for you. There is a difference."

"No killing! No killing of anyone, anywhere! Is that clear?" I fell to my knees and hovered protectively over Peter, who watched with huge eyes as the sword tip waved back and forth over his face. "And while you're at it, call your buddies off my friends!"

Eirik frowned, giving me a blue-eyed glare. "You are a

strange goddess. You do not want us to kill anyone in your name, and you will not allow my men a little fun . . . what is next? You will not allow us to have a *spritfest* and wench and gamble?"

"*Spritfest*?"

"Drinking party."

"Ah, OK. I don't care about drinking and . . . er . . . whatever else you do so long as it's not trying to kill anyone," I said, glaring back at him.

Eirik snarled something under his breath, but pulled back his sword. "As you command," he said in a grumpy voice.

I blinked a couple of times, not sure whether he was kidding me or not, but it turned out he meant what he said.

"You're serious about this whole goddess thing, aren't you?" I asked, patting Peter on the shoulder to know he could sit up. He did so as I got to my feet. I helped him brush off the bits of dirt and dried grass.

Eirik shrugged. "You are a goddess. We are bound to you until you call the Valkyries to take us to Valhalla."

"In that case . . ." I stopped brushing Peter's back and jumped onto the nearest picnic table. I put two fingers in my mouth to do the ear-splitting whistle my dad was famous for. "Vikings!" I bellowed, and to my surprise, they stopped catapulting, fighting, climbing, and groping.

Mikaela kicked Finnvid in his happy zone. He doubled over and fell to the ground.

"Right, Eirik says you have to listen to me and do what I say. So, I'm saying knock it off! There will be no killing anyone! No hurling of fruit, peaches or otherwise.

71

No climbing on any furniture in an attempt to get to someone."

Finnvid writhed on the ground. Mikaela emptied her water bottle on him, and rushed over to help Ramon up from the mass of peach pulp.

"No picking up women."

A huge Viking with long blond hair walked around the corner with Soren slung over his shoulder.

"In fact, no picking up anyone!"

"Hail, Ljot," Eirik called to his buddy. "The goddess is giving us orders."

"Oh?" Ljot, the giant Viking, turned to face me, a happy smile on his face. Soren's legs kicked feebly. "Who do we kill?"

"Sheesh, what is it with you guys?" I asked, slapping my hands on my thighs in exasperation. "Don't you know how to do anything other than fight and kill people? And put down Soren—he doesn't look like he's breathing."

The Vikings, every single one of them, looked thoughtful. Ljot the friendly giant plopped Soren into a lawn chair. "We wench well," one of them offered.

"Aye, that we do, Gils," Eirik agreed, and all the Vikings nodded (except Finnvid, who was struggling to get to his knees, his hands clasped over his groin). "And we can outdrink anyone, even a Finn."

The Vikings yelled their war cry. I squatted next to Soren and asked him if he was OK.

"Yes, I'm fine. Just a little windy," he said, rubbing his ribs.

"Winded, I think you mean. Windy means something else." I stood up again and looked at the Viking ghosts, my hands on my hips. "All right, so we need to have some ground rules—"

"I can geld stallions with just one hand," one of the Vikings said. The others looked impressed.

"Ew!" I said, giving him a glare. "I don't know who you are—"

"His name is Isleif," Eirik said helpfully, strolling over to stand next to me.

"—but that's just gross. Moving on . . . you're all going to have to behave yourselves, or else I'll . . . I'll . . ."

Eririk raised an eyebrow. "You'll what?"

"I won't call the Valkyries to take you to Valhalla," I said. "So everyone had just better straighten up, OK?"

"What is she talking about?" one of the shorter Vikings asked another.

"We're supposed to be good," the second Viking answered with a disgusted look on his face.

"That sucks," the first answered.

I raised an eyebrow at him. "Sucks?"

"Just because we're dead doesn't mean we don't keep current on what's going on in the world, goddess," Eirik answered. "Would you like to see us line dance?"

"No!" I shuddered to myself. "Just . . . behave, OK? I'm working on getting you to Valhalla as soon as I can. I just need to figure out how to summon the Valkyries first. Hopefully, that'll be before tomorrow night."

The Vikings looked disapointed, a couple of them pouting, but they did as I asked.

"Why tomorrow night?" Eirik asked as his men started cleaning up the mess they'd made. Peter gave Eirik a wide berth as he went to check on Soren.

"That's when I have—" Everyone, and I do mean everyone—from Absinthe climbing down off her trailer to Ramon, who was helping Mikaela pick off sticky blobs of peach—stopped what they were doing and looked at me. It was like a TV commercial or something. "Er . . . I have a thing I'm doing."

"A thing?" Eirik frowned, scratching his chin with the handle of his sword. "What sort of thing?"

"Kind of a date," I said as quietly as I could. I may have to live and work with these people—the ghosts aside—but they didn't need to know every little thing about me.

"A date?" Eirik asked in a voice that could probably be heard in Denmark. "You have a date? You mean with the Dark One?"

"You're going on a date with Benedikt?" Soren asked, limping over, an odd expression on his face. Peter went to check on his sister and the others. "A real date? Not just hanging around with him?"

I sighed. "Yes, I'm going on a date, a real date."

"The kind where you—" he waved his hands around vaguely—"do things?"

"How do I know? I've never been on a date before!" I said, just wishing everyone would leave me alone. Honestly, it was just a date!

"You've never been on a date before?" Eirik asked, pulling up a chair. "You need advice." He said something in what I assumed was ancient Viking to the others. They stopped what they were doing and made a circle around me. "The goddess is going on a date. Her *first* date."

"Ahh," the Vikings all said, looking at me like I was a boar about to be roasted.

"A first date. That is very important," the one named Isleif said. He was just as tall as the rest, but really big around, as well. Unlike most of them, he also had a beard, the sides of which were done up in a braid. He plopped down on another chair and put his hands on his knees. "I will give you the same advice I gave my daughter Anna."

"This I *have* to hear," Soren said, his arms across his chest as he gave me a belligerant look. I wanted to tell him to knock it off, too, but I didn't. I've never had a crush before—Ben aside, and he wasn't exactly a crush— but I imagined it wasn't a good feeling if the person you were crushing didn't feel the same way about you.

"I appreciate the offer for advice, but I don't really think I need—"

" 'Anna,' I told her—you understand this was close to nine hundred years ago, but you girls never change— 'Anna,' I said, 'you are twelve now, ready to be wed. Your skin is the color of the richest curd, your teeth are strong enough to tear a leather thong, and your breasts are like two little apples, ripe for the plucking.' Then I told her—"

"Twelve?" Soren interrupted, looking shocked.

"OK, no plucking stories," I said, waving my hands for Isleif to stop. "Dating advice from a Viking ghost I can just barely survive, but no apple plucking! I don't want to hear anything about your daughter's boobs."

Isleif looked insulted. "They were very nice. High and firm and—" I started to walk away. Isleif yelled for me to stop. "I have not finished! As I said, I told Anna the time was right for her to be wed. I had always intended that she marry Ljot's son, but he went and got himself killed by a mad boar. Ljot had another son, but he was a bit light in the head."

"Daft." Ljot nodded. "No brains whatsoever. He got that from his mother."

"Anna insisted she be allowed to look around for a husband," Isleif continued. "But she didn't know how to proceed with the one she'd chosen. So I told her—and this is the wisdom I'm passing along to you—the best way to catch yourself a husband is to rip his clothing off, and have your way with him." Isleif sat back, a pleased look on his face like he'd just explained the greatest mystery of the universe.

"Um," I said, not wanting to insult him. The other Vikings were nodding their agreement.

"That's how my second wife caught me," Finnvid said. "She followed me to the lake one summer morn, wrestled me to the ground, stripped me naked, and sat—"

"Thanks for the advice," I said really loudly, giving Finnvid a look that he evidently didn't get, because he just grinned at me. "I'll . . . uh . . . take it into consideration."

"You're not really going to rip Benedikt's clothes off, are you?" Soren asked a few seconds later as I was walking back toward my trailer.

"Of course not! I'm brand new to this whole girlfriend thing. There's no way I'd attempt as advanced a technique as clothes-ripping-off."

Soren shot me a questioning look from the corner of his eye. "You're joking, *ja?*"

"Yes, I'm joking." I stopped at the steps to the trailer. "Honest, Soren, it's not a big deal. Ben and I are going out on a date, just a date. Probably dinner and a movie. No biggie at all."

Soren didn't say anything, but his eyes were troubled. I didn't know what I could say to him that was the truth and yet would help him over the crush, so I didn't say anything. I socked him on the shoulder and told him he could help me find Tesla.

"I thought you and Benedikt already looked for him?" he asked, socking me back.

"We did. But I was thinking last night—here we are in a fair full of people with all sorts of freaky powers, and I'm not using any of it."

"You touched the hobble," he pointed out.

"Yeah, but that didn't tell me much. I'm going to see if Tallulah can tell me anything."

"She's a medium, not a diviner. What you need is someone who can tell you where to find Tesla."

"Tallulah has Sir Edward. She says he can see every-thing from the Akashic Plain."

"The what?" Soren's nose scrunched up in confusion.

"Akashic Plain. It's kind of like limbo. Imogen told me about it last week. I'm going to see Tallulah later. You want to come?"

"Sure, if I have my chores done."

"No prob. My mom should be back any minute, and then I'm going to have to spend some time dealing with leaving her circle last night. I'm lucky she didn't slap the itching spell on me this morning."

Soren trotted off and I used the next half hour to wash and get dressed, taking a few minutes to scarf down some green tea, toast, and two apples. I felt at twinge at the last one, since I automatically set one aside for Tesla. "Poor old boy. I hope you're all right," I said just as the door opened and my mother came into the trailer.

"Oh good, you're up," she said, a glint in her eye warning she was going to read me the lecture of a lifetime for leaving her circle before she'd broken it. She plopped down her bag of Wiccan stuff on the table, along with a familiar nylon object. "I found this halter in the clearing. I assume it was Tesla's."

I burst into tears. I know what you're thinking, but it wasn't an attempt to distract Mom from the lecture—just the sight of seeing the halter I'd bought him before we left Hungary broke my heart, driving home the point that some stranger had my horse. "I don't know where he is," I said in between sobs as Mom tried to comfort me, murmuring things about it being all right. "I don't know who has him, or if he's hungry, or in pain, or being made to walk too much—you know he's not supposed to get anything but a little gentle exercise! He's too old for a lot of running around. He could be dead and I wouldn't . . . wouldn't . . ." I couldn't go on. It was too horrible to think about.

"Aw, honey, I know it's hard, but you really can't believe the worst. If this Lars Laufeyiarson person wanted Tesla enough to offer you so much money for him, he's not going to be abused or mistreated."

"But we can't find Lars Laufeyiarson," I said, sniffling into a couple of tissues. Yes, it was stupid to cry, but sometimes you just have to give in and have a good sobfest. "We checked all the phone books in the area. There are a couple up the coast, but Ben called them and they weren't the same guy."

Mom frowned. "I thought he gave you his card? What happened to that?"

"It disappeared."

She gave me a look.

"No, I'm serious, it disappeared. I put it in my bag when I got back to the trailer that night, and when I went to look last night, it was gone. Poof. Vanished into nothing."

"Or someone took it," she said slowly, shaking her head as soon as she spoke. "No, no one would come into our trailer and touch our things. You must have lost it or misplaced it somewhere, honey."

I bit my lip to keep from telling her I distinctly remembered putting it in my purse where it would be safe. Although Mom was Wiccan and had seen all sorts of strange things, she never believed any of them could happen to me.

"Now, about you leaving the circle last night—"

I sat back and let her give me the old "why it's wrong to leave a circle" lecture, glancing out of the open window when I thought I heard someone calling my name. There was no one out there but one of the Viking ghosts sweeping up peach debris. I nodded at the appropriate times, shaking my head when that was called for, looking out the window again when I could have sworn someone was calling me.

"—and to think you'd been raised to honor and re-

spect our practices. I was appalled by your abrupt—
Franny, I am speaking to you. I would appreciate having
your attention." Mom stopped her pacing up and down
to glare at me, her hands on her hips.

"Sorry. I thought someone was calling me," I said,
hurriedly turning back toward her and putting on my
"being lectured yet again" face.

Fran, the wind whispered.

"Honestly, Fran, I have no idea what you thought you
were doing—"

I tuned her out to listen as hard as I could for the elu-
sive sound.

Fran.

Ben?

Fran. You . . . help . . .

"Absolutely," I said, leaping to my feet and heading
for the door. "I'm so sorry about the circle, Mom. Never
happen again. Promise. Gotta run now."

"Francesca Marie Ghetti—"

"Sorry, sorry, sorry," I yelled as I flung myself out of the
trailer, running toward the center aisle of the Faire, stopping to get my bearings. *Ben, where are you?*

Woods, the answer came in kind of a gasp. My heart
leaped at the sound of it—Ben was in trouble, serious
trouble if he was asking for help. Part of his Mister Macho act was that he never, ever asked for help from anyone. *West.*

I raced down the aisle, ignoring the shouted question
from Soren as he tended to Bruno, past Tallulah as she
took her pug for a walk, down the slope that led to the
parking area, and into the sparse fringe of woods that ran

like a spine down the center of the small island. *Ben? Whereabouts are you? I don't see you.*

Here, a faint voice whispered in my head. *Left.*

I spun around and ran into the woods, beating back stray branches as they slapped at my face. I figured he wouldn't be at the edge, where the sunshine could get him, so I went for the darkest part of the thin stretch of woods. I wouldn't have seen him slumped up against a giant fir tree if he hadn't moved, but fortunately I caught the movement in my peripheral vision. "What's wrong? Why are you hiding in the trees? Where have you—oh, goddess! What's happened to you?"

My skin tightened and tingled with goose bumps as Ben slumped to the ground. He wore the tattered remains of his leather jacket, his shirt completely gone, but that wasn't what made my stomach freeze into a solid block of horror—his face, arms, and torso was bright red with blood, as if he'd been dipped in a blood bath. Beneath it, I could see a horrifying crisscross pattern of slash marks on his chest and arms. I lunged for him but couldn't catch him as he hit the ground, his head lolling backward. I touched his throat, feeling for a pulse, but there was nothing. His chest didn't rise with breath. His heart didn't beat. And his being, his self that I was always subtly aware of when he was around, was utterly and completely gone.

I sat on the ground, clutching his lifeless body to me, my mind shrieking in horror. How on earth was I going to go on without Ben?

CHAPTER SEVEN

"I'm never going to forgive you for this," I said, throwing a pillow down onto the floor.

An eye the color of dark oak opened and rolled over to look at me for a second or two before closing again.

"You've died twice in my arms. Twice! There's not going to be a third time, do you understand?"

The man-shaped lump on the bed grunted.

"Dark Ones can't die unless they're beheaded," Imogen said, bustling into the bedroom of her trailer with yet another jar of cow's blood (I know, major ick, but this was an emergency). She stopped for a moment and looked thoughtful. "Or burned—they can be burned, too. And if they lose all the blood in their body, that's as good as dead since they are more or less comatose. But they can't die just from a few cuts."

I glared at her for a moment, before looking over to where Ben lay, swathed in bandages, propped up on a pyramid of pillows. He looked awful, his skin gaunt and gray as if he was every single one of his three hundred and twelve years. He'd lost so much blood, Imogen couldn't replace what he needed, so she had sent Karl into town to buy some blood from the local butcher.

Imogen sat on the edge of the bed, tucking a blanket around his hips. She was about to offer him the mug when she looked over to me. "Do you want to do this, Fran?"

"I'm sorry, I can't," I said, throwing another pillow around. I picked up Ben's bloodstained jeans and shook them at him. "I'm too busy being furious at him to pour blood down his throat."

Ben opened his eye again and looked at his sister. "She's picking on me."

"As you well deserve. I can't imagine what you were thinking collapsing like that on poor Fran. You scared her to death! You should have seen her face when she came dashing back here to get help for you. She was devestated, her face the very picture of horror and agony. I wanted to weep just seeing the despair in her eyes."

Ben looked at me. "You were that worried about me?"

"Yes, I was." I picked up his bloody, shredded jacket, narrowing my eyes at him. "That was a horrible, horrible thing you did to me! And I'm telling you right here and now that I'm never going to go through that again! No more, got that? No more scaring Fran to death! Twice is enough, thank you!"

"The first time wasn't my fault," he protested in a weak voice that just about broke my heart. "I'm not to blame if a demon tried to kill me."

"I suppose it really wasn't his fault last month," Imogen said, thrusting the mug of blood at Ben. He shot her a narrow-eyed look, but obediently sipped at the blood. I was glad Imogen knew what to do for him—when I had staggered back into our camp earlier, my brain was frozen solid, locked on the thought that he was dead. I had no idea what to do to help him—assuming help was possible. But thankfully, Imogen took charge of the situation immediately, helping Kurt to bring Ben back while Karl went for some take-out blood.

"Maybe not directly, but he was pig-headed enough to get himself ambushed."

"Pig-headed!" Ben sputtered around the mug.

"That's what I said. Are you done?" I asked when he pushed Imogen's hand holding the mug away.

"Yes."

He didn't look much better, but at least he'd had a couple of pints of blood, and his wounds had stopped bleeding. "Good. Now you can tell us what happened to you."

The silent, stony look I received was a familiar one.

"Oh, no," I said, hands on hips again (I seemed to be doing that a lot lately). "You're not going to give me the silent treatment. I order you to tell me what happened to you."

Ben glared. Imogen made a little face. "Fran, dear, a word of advice—never give Benedikt an order. He doesn't like them."

"I'm not one of your ghosts, Fran," he said, having finished his glare. "You cannot compel me to tell you where I've been."

"I can't, huh?" I sat on the bed, stripped off a glove, and took his hand in mine. His fingers, as always, fascinated me. They were long and slender, the hands of a musician. These hands had been around for more than three hundred years, buttoning fancy Victorian waistcoats, loading muskets, holding on to the side of a sleek, polished carriage—and so many other things, I couldn't even begin to imagine. And yet with all that history behind them, they were just hands, warm, supportive hands that gave me a little zing of pleasure each time they touched me. "What if I ask you to please tell me what happened? What if I remind you that I was absolutely devestated when I saw you so weak and injured." *What if I let you see how much it broke my heart to think you were gone?*

He closed his eyes for a minute, his fingers tightening around mine. "I was helping my brother."

My eyebrows shot up in surprise. "You have a brother?"

Imogen shook her head.

"Dafydd is my blood brother, not an actual relation. He saved my life once. I am bound to return that debt." Ben's eyes were still shut, but his thumb stroked over mine. A little warm glow of happiness filled me at his touch, joining with the massive well of relief and gratitude that he hadn't died.

"Oh. What exactly were you helping him with?"

He shook his head. "That I cannot tell you. I swore an oath of secrecy to him."

"Poop. Well, how were you hurt? Those slash marks were deep and jagged, like something with really big claws got you."

His eyes were dark when they opened, the lovely little sparkly gold bits dull and flat. "I can't tell you that, either."

"What *can* you tell me?" It took an effort, but I managed to keep from strangling him. Long exposure to Wiccans had taught me the importance of honoring an oath, although that didn't make it any easier on me when I was dying to know what happened to him.

He said nothing.

I counted to ten. "OK, how about this—does whatever you're doing tonight have to do with you disappearing in Hungary last month?"

"Yes."

I don't know why, but that actually made me feel a bit better. Not that I was jealous or anything, but I wouldn't be human if I didn't admit that a couple of times, the horrible thought had occurred to me that Ben might have taken off with someone much thinner, smaller, and all around less weird. But if he was off helping his blood brother . . . well that, too, I could understand. Wiccans are very big on bonds of blood.

I sighed. "OK. I won't ask you any more about that. But this obviously means our date tomorrow is off."

"Date?" Imogen asked, puttering around the tiny bedroom. She fluffed up one of Ben's pillows, tucked the sheet around him tighter, and readjusted a curtain so the tendril of sunshine that sneaked in was eliminated. Her eyes went from me to Ben and back. "You two are going on a date? A real one?"

"We were. Dinner and everything." I gave Ben's hand a final squeeze as I stood up. He needed to rest and let his body heal all those horrible wounds, and me sitting there wouldn't do him any good. "But now we'll have to wait until he's better."

"I'll be fine by tomorrow night," he said, giving me a feeble smile.

"Uh huh."

"I will. I should be back to normal tonight, as a matter of fact."

I made a face that let him know I thought that was a bit optimistic, told him to get some sleep, and left Imogen's bedroom.

"Oh, Francesca . . ." She followed me out of the bedroom, carefully closing the door behind her. Her forehead was wrinkled with a puzzled frown. "About this date . . ."

"What about it?" I asked.

"It's just . . . you've never been on a date before, have you? I seem to recall you telling me that."

"Yeah, but it's not like I have to pass a test or anything to do it."

She met my smile with one of her own. "No, but I thought you mightn't mind a little advice."

"Sure," I said, taking a seat at the semicircular table. "I'd be happy to get some advice from the queen of dating. It has to be better than what the Vikings told me."

"Tea?" She bustled around the tiny kitchen area.

"Just a fast one. I have to visit Tallulah, and then give Tibolt his necklace back."

She paused for a moment at the mention of Tibolt, sighed heavily, then shook her head and reached for the electric tea kettle she had plugged in earlier. "I wouldn't quite call myself a queen of dating—just someone who has learned a few good tips over the centuries. First, you naturally want to ensure is that your date worships you as is your due."

"Uh . . ." I thought about Ben arguing with me.

"That is not a problem with Benedikt, as you are his Beloved."

That had me laughing a little as I sipped the cup of Earl Grey she set down in front of me. "I may be his Beloved, but I don't think *worship* is the word I'd use about his feelings. More like pushy and bossy, although admittedly really, really hot."

"That aside, you must remember what you are owed. Allow him to open doors for you, and pull out your chair. Beyond that, just smile. If something doesn't please you, don't ruin the evening by whining—just keep smiling and ignore the problem. And above all, don't resist if Benedikt wishes to give you a memento of the evening."

I opened my mouth to tell her there was no way I'd do half the stuff she said, but stopped because I knew she was trying to be helpful. "Memento?" I asked, instead. "What sort of memento? Like a picture or something?"

"Oh, goodness no. Something sparkly," she answered, absently turning the sapphire tennis bracelet on her wrist. "Benedikt has excellent taste in jewelry. You may trust him to pick out something that will be in style for many, many years."

I choked on my tea at the thought of letting Ben buy me jewelry. He'd already given me his mother's ring, and my mother just about had a hissy at that. I couldn't imagine what she would do if he gave me anything sparkly. Not to mention I wasn't a sparkly kind of girl.

"Well, thanks for that advice. It's very helpful," I said

without even giggling, getting up to set my cup in the tiny sink. "I have to run now. I'm hoping to catch Talullah before she goes to town. Let me know if you need help with Ben."

"You'll remember what I said?" she asked, coming to the door as I hurried down the couple of steps.

"Absolutely. Sparkly. Smile. No whining."

She beamed back at me. "It'll be a lovely date, Fran. I just know it will."

I was a bit less optomistic, but I still waved cheerily to her as I trotted toward Talullah's trailer. Soren was still busy, so I was on my own with Talullah.

Even though she was older than my mother, Talullah had a little blue Vespa that she used to zoom around wherever we were staying, strapping Wennie the pug into a basket on the front of the scooter so he wouldn't fall out and get run over.

I found her just leaving her trailer, her shopping bag tucked under one arm, Wennie in his lightweight travel jacket in the other.

"Good morning," she said, her black eyes carefully looking me over. "I see you have your ghosts under control at last."

"Yeah, well, I didn't know they were going to cause any trouble." I'd given up trying to get everyone to realize the ghosts didn't belong to me. Evidently everyone, including the Vikings themselves, thought they did. "I'm sorry you were attacked with peaches."

She looked at me silently for a moment, then turned back and opened the door to her trailer. "You wish for me to conduct a reading."

"Yeah, if you don't mind. I know you're about to leave, but I promise it won't take long."

"I am happy to help you," she said primly, and sat on a bench couch that was almost identical to ours. "You have been troubled of late. I have not been pleased to see that. You are young, too young to be burdened with the cares you have."

"Like Viking ghosts?" I asked, taking a seat when she waved toward the opposite end of the couch. Talullah was a gypsy queen—at least, that's what my mother said—and looking at her I could believe it. It was hard to tell exactly how old she was, although her jet black hair had a streak of white slightly off center. It wasn't her appearance that always made me feel slightly uncomfortable, like I'd been called into the principal's office to find out what I was in trouble for . . . it was the natural dignity and grace that she wore almost as an aura that made me believe the rumors that she had been a powerful queen in a Romany tribe, but had abdicated to lead a quieter life.

"Pfft," she said, pulling out a small flat black bowl. Its surface was mirrored, so shiny I could see the details of every line in her face as she set it down before her. "The ghosts are not what is troubling you. Your auras are muddy, but I can see that at least one thing is giving you much concern."

"One?" I would've thought there'd be two—Ben and Tesla—but then I realized I wasn't really worried about Ben anymore. I knew he would recover just fine. "Yeah, I guess just the one thing. But—auras? Plural? I thought I just had one?"

"That is a common misconception. You can manifest up to five auras under the right circumstances, but most people only show three. Have you never been to the aura photography booth?"

I shook my head. "I never really wanted to know."

One of her eyebrows rose in question. "I see. Well, I will save you the trouble by telling you now that your inner aura is white, indicating purity and chasteness, your middle aura is blue, indicating disatisfaction with something in your life, and your outer aura is a sharp red, all of which tells me that you have a pure heart, are on the beginning of a path to enlightenment, but your energies now are focused on the problem which troubles you."

"Tesla," I said, sighing.

"Ah, your horse that was stolen?" She nodded and tilted the shallow black mirror bowl so she could look into it. "Let us consult Sir Edward and see what he has to say about Tesla."

When Mom first dragged me to the GothFaire a month ago—committing us to traveling around with them for half a year—I made the big mistake of asking Talullah why she didn't use a crystal ball like a normal medium. Her response still made me squirm uncomfortably—she had pinned me back with a glare and said in a voice that had the faintest touch of an accent, "I am *not* normal. Normal is for lesser people."

Although I didn't diss normal the way she did, I couldn't dispute the fact that she seemed perfectly happy the way she was. I watched her now as she hummed softly to herself, swaying slightly, her eyes fixed on the bowl. It never failed to amaze me how normal everyone looked on the outside, but inside they had some really jaw-dropping abilities.

"Sir Edward is with us," she said suddenly in a singsong voice.

"Oh, good. Hi, Sir Edward."

A little breeze whispered by me. I got goose bumps from it even knowing that Sir Edward was a good spirit.

"He is pleased to see you, although he, too, notes that you are troubled, and is displeased by that."

"Sorry about that. I'll try to be less . . . er . . . troubled."

The Sir Edward breeze gently touched my face. "He wishes to help you with your troubles. What do you wish to ask him?"

"I want to know where Tesla is. I want to know who took him, and why, and whether Tesla is OK."

The breeze caressing me stilled for a moment, then went whipping past me with enough velocity to ruffle my hair.

"Oh," Tallulah said, her eyes distant and unseeing as she maintained her trance by staring into the bowl.

"Uh . . . oh?"

"Yes. Sir Edward is distraught. He is not making sense. One moment while I commune with him."

I sat quietly while she stared into the bowl. The only sound in the trailer came from Wennie as he snored, stretched out on his belly next to her.

"Ahhhh," Talullah said on a long sigh, blinking as she came out of the trance. She set the bowl down and gave me a long look.

Despite my best intentions, tears pricked behind my

eyes. Something was wrong with Tesla, I just knew it. "He's hurt?"

She shook her head.

I swallowed back a big lump in my throat and croaked out the next word. "Dead?"

"No. Fran, do not weep. I do not know how Tesla is— Sir Edward could not see him."

"He couldn't?" I sniffed and used the back of my hand to wipe off a couple of sneaky tears. "Why couldn't he see him? I thought Sir Edward was a scout or something."

"Guide, he is a spirit guide, which means he exists in the Akashic Plain and can see all, but this even he could not divine."

"Why?" I felt slightly better, although my worry level increased a few hundred notches.

"He said the vision of Tesla was blocked, hidden by a being much more powerful than he had seen before."

My skin crawled, I swear it positively crawled up my arms. "What sort of a being?"

"Sir Edward did not know. It was not a being he has encountered before." The look she gave me was long and full of unspoken warning. "But he did say the being seems to have great power, and it would be the sheerest folly for you to pursue it. I'm afraid for all intents and purposes that your horse is lost to you, Fran. To attempt to regain it from this being would likely result in your death."

Chapter Eight

There's nothing that ticks me off more than being told I can't do something. I'm not talking about obviously stupid things like walking out in front of a moving semi truck, but things like "Don't stay up late on a school night," "Don't go swimming right after eating," and most of all, "Don't try to get your elderly horse back from the weirdo being who stole him from you."

I'm not an idiot, however. "If Sir Edward was scared by Mr. Laufeyiarson—assuming he was the one who stole Tesla, and it's not likely he is a coincidence—then that meant Mr. Laufeyiarson isn't what he appeared. Then again, who *is* around here?"

Soren nodded. We were perched on a fallen tree, watching Bruno graze by the light of the afternoon sun. I had a few painful minutes when I had a little pity party about Tesla not being there, but one thing I've learned—crying about something seldom makes it change. Therefore, it was up to me to find Tesla, and get him back.

"That's true." Soren chewed one of the curried

chicken sandwiches I'd made for us both, picking out the bits of celery, which he didn't like. "But if a ghost is scared of him . . . well, that says something, right?"

"Kind of. It says I'm going to need some help getting Tesla back." I popped a couple green grapes in my mouth and wondered whether Ben really was going to be well enough to go on the date tomorrow night. I'd already done the angsting over my wardrobe—I had exactly one skirt—and managed to beg a little spending money from Mom for a trip into town. "But that's one of the benefits of having a vampire for a boyfriend. Ben will help me tackle Mr. Laufeyiarson. They had something going on earlier, when he tried to buy Tesla. Ben never did tell me what Laufeyiarson said to him."

"Maybe Benedikt is in on the theft," Soren said, his eyes narrowing. "Maybe that was a setup."

"Why do you insist on calling Ben by his full name?" I asked, tipping my head to the side to look at Soren. "Imogen does, but she's his sister, and you know how it is with family. But no one else calls him Benedikt. Well, OK, my mom does sometimes, but she has that whole mom thing going on. Why do you do it?"

Soren shrugged and looked away. "When are you going into town?"

"As soon as Imogen is ready." I smiled to myself about the quick change of subject. "You want to come?"

"I should give Bruno another bath, but he had one three days ago," Soren said, looking indecisive for a moment. "Meh. I will go with you two. If Papa is mad, he's mad. It's not as if he can fire me."

"Vive la résistance," I said, having watched an old black-and-white movie called *Casablanca* the other night with Imogen.

"Ja. What did Tibolt say about the necklace?"

I stuffed the last bit of sandwich in my mouth and dusted off my hands before pulling out the pendant from where it lay beneath my T-shirt. "He didn't. I couldn't find him this morning. Ramon said he was off communing with the gods, which Mikaela snarked meant he was working on his tan. I didn't want to disturb him, so I'll just catch him tonight."

"Snarked?" Soren's face wrinkled as he tried to figure out the word.

"It means said snarkily. You know, kind of smart ass. Not quite mean, but not nice, either. Snarked."

"Ah. You are good for my vocabulary." He tossed a couple of grapes in the air and tried to catch them in his mouth. They bounced off his face and rolled into the grass. "If all he is doing is lying in the sun, you could ask him to take the necklace back."

"No, I don't think so," I said, smiling.

"Ah? Why not?"

"Because evidently he's working on an all-over tan." Soren blinked at me in confusion for a moment. "You know, nude sunbathing?"

"Oh!" His eyes got big as he nodded. "No, you do not want to disturb him. I'm surprised that Imogen isn't with him."

My smile turned to a grin. "Evidently Desdemona beat her to it. Imogen had a couple of really interesting things to say about that, but in the end she decided to go shopping rather than duke it out with Desdemona."

"Ah."

"Anyway, Mikaela said Tibolt would be back around supper time, so I can catch him—oh, there's Imogen. Let's get this over with."

"I thought most girls liked to shop?" he asked as we followed Imogen to the parking area.

I tipped my chin up so I could look down my nose at him, doing my best to sound like Tallulah. "*I* am not most girls."

He snorted as we approached Imogen's white car. "You can say that again."

I punched him in the arm.

"Goddess! Where are you going?"

I stopped and glanced over my shoulder at where Eirik was yelling at me. He and Finnvid and Isleif were squatting around a small fire, roasting something that looked like it had once been a cute little bunny. I decided I really, really didn't want to know, so I kept my eyes on Eirik. "Shopping with Imogen."

"Shopping?" He frowned for a moment, then said something to the other two. Finnvid jumped up immediately, Isleif waiting before he pulled the dead thing off the makeshift spit before following the other two. "We will come with you."

"Um," I said, not wanting to offend them, but not particularly wanting an audience of Vikings while I tried on dresses. "Imogen's car is kind of small."

"Not that small," Finnvid said with a knowing smile. I

figured that was just something else I didn't want to know.

Imogen raised her eyebrows as we approached. "You gentlemen are all coming with us?"

"Yes. We wish to shop." Eirik took the front seat. I guess he figured that as head Viking, he got to ride shotgun. "There are many things we need."

"Er . . . I don't think there's enough room for everyone," I said, looking at Soren, Finnvid, Isleif, and the backseat.

"You may sit on me," Isleif said. "You are big, but I am bigger."

I bit my tongue fighting back the urge to snap back something mean about his "you are big" comment.

"Soren will sit on Finnvid," Eirik said, playing with the air conditioner. "He is small, and Finnvid won't mind."

"I am not sitting on anyone!" Soren said, backing away as Finnvid tried to grab him.

"You can sit up front, between Eirik and me," Imogen told him, pushing him toward the front seat.

"There, you see? Everyone fits. Let us go," Eirik said. "Are we going to McDonald's again, as well? Last night Isleif ate ten Big Macs. I will show him that I can eat eleven."

I sighed, wondering if anyone else ever got stuck with Viking ghosts that were addicted to McDonald's. I climbed onto Isleif's lap, apologizing to Finnvid when I inadvertantly kicked him in the knee. I didn't mind sitting on Isleif because he had a daughter my age—or he did at one point, several hundred years ago—but it was a tight fit getting the two big Vikings and me into the back of Imogen's car.

"What exactly—oh, sorry again, Finnvid. My foot was cramping—what exactly do you guys want to buy?" I asked as we crossed the causeway over to the mainland. The town of Benlös Vessla was just a few minutes away, a nice enough place with a couple of streets of shops, suburbs, even a couple strip malls.

"Finnvid wishes to visit Kärleksgrottan," Eirik answered, leaning back as the air conditioning blew on him.

"Kärleksgrottan?" I asked.

"Yes. It means love grotto. Finnvid has heard of something called a motion lotion, and wishes to try it."

I peeked at Imogen. She was blushing faintly, but kept her eyes on the road and said nothing. I added Finnvid's quest to my Too Much Information list.

"I wish to get a new bow," Isleif rumbled behind me. "I have seen pictures of modern bows in a catalog. I want one with a laser sight. No moose would ever escape me then!"

"Er . . . I don't think hunting is allowed now," I said, crossing my fingers because I had no idea whether or not that was true. I just didn't want to see Isleif hauling in the corpse of a moose some morning.

"It isn't? What is this country coming to?" Isleif grumbled under his breath for a few seconds. "Then I will get a new hunting knife. A sharp one, with a compass in the handle."

Soren turned around just enough to raise his eyebrows at me. I shook my head slightly, telling him it was useless to get into a lecture against hunting with guys who spent their entire lives doing it.

"And I wish to get a Game Boy," Eirik said, his eyes still closed, a look of bliss on his face as he wallowed in the cold air blowing from the front vent. "I have seen many tourists with them. I wish to blow up tiny little people as they do."

Soren snickered.

"It sounds like you guys will be busy for a while buying all your stuff."

"Buying?" Finnvid asked. "We do not buy. We are Vikings! We pillage!"

"Pillaging is also outlawed now," Imogen said, winking at Finnvid in the rearview mirror. "You must buy things or the police will lock you away in a very small room. It is not pleasant."

"You don't have any money?" I asked Eirik, who was sitting up now, looking around the town as Imogen drove us down the main street.

He frowned. "No. We will barter."

"Barter what?" I asked, chewing on my lower lip. I didn't want the ghosts glommed onto me forever, but neither did I want to see them end up in jail for shoplifting.

"We have gold and silver," Finnvid said nonchalantly, rolling down his window in order to stick his head out of it.

"Oh. Well that should do. OK, so you guys do your bartering thing while Imogen and Soren help me pick out a dress, and then we'll all head back to the Faire in time for the opening."

"A dress?" Eirik asked, his head swivelling around to look at me.

"For your date with the Dark One?" Finnvid asked.

"Yeah, but—"

"We will help you pick out a dress. This date, it is important to you." Eirik pointed out an empty space in the parking lot. "Vikings have good taste. You will trust our opinion."

"I will?" I asked, unfolding my legs to get out of the car. My left foot had gone numb, causing me to do a little pins-and-needles dance. "Uh . . . Imogen has had a lot more experience picking out clothes, and she said she'd help me first, so it's only fair—"

"Bah," Eirik said, grabbing my arm and hustling me down the sidewalk. I have to give the people in Benlös Vessla credit—they didn't bat a single eyelash at the sight of three Vikings walking around town. Imogen was giggling with Finnvid behind us as I was marched between Eirik and Isleif to a ladies' clothing shop. Soren rolled his eyes and followed. "Imogen is a woman and thus does not have as much good taste as we do. In this, we are superior. We are Vikings!"

"That's what you said about killing people and stuff," I said, resisting as best I could even though I knew it wouldn't do me any good. I was right. Isleif and Eirik just pushed me into the shop.

"We are superior in all things," Eirik said, looking around the store. Soren wandered in, found himself directly in front of a table mounded high with panties, gawked at them with a horrified look on his face, and ran to the other side of the store.

"Finnvid, fetch the slave—"

"Sales assistant," I corrected, spying a middle-aged lady in the back of the shop that I took to be the owner or a sales person.

"—to attend the goddess. We will pick out something for you. You sit until we're ready."

"I don't *think* so," I said to their backs as they went over to a rack of dresses. A few seconds later, I had to apologize profusely when Finnvid plopped down the sales lady he'd picked up and carried from the back of the store. "I'm so sorry. My . . . *friends* . . . are a little enthusiastic. Do you speak English?"

"Yes," the woman said in a heavy accent, her eyes huge as she looked from Finnvid to Eirik and Isleif. Luckily, there wasn't anyone else in the shop. "Yes, I do. Er . . . you wish to buy something?"

"These are charming lace panties," Imogen said, coming up with a handful of underwear. "Do you have matching bras? I do like my undergarments to match."

"Yes, behind you," the woman said, nodding toward the chair into which Soren had slumped. He looked even more horrified as he followed the woman's gaze and turned his head to find a wall of bras next to him.

"I'll be outside," he said quickly, dashing for the door.

"Sales slave! Do you have nothing with ermine or squirrel?" Eirik called, holding a horrible slinky purple disco dress.

"Er . . ." the sales woman said, her mouth hanging open slightly.

"I've found it works best if you just ignore them," I told

her in a quiet voice. "They really do mean well, but they can be a bit much if you let yourself think about them."

"Er . . ."

"The goddess has a date with a Dark One. She must be dressed according to her station," Finnvid said, holding up a pair of moss green linen capris to his waist as he checked his reflection in the mirror.

"Eh . . ." The sales lady looked like she wanted to bolt.

"Fran, you must come look at these lace bras. They are extremely well made. I'm sure if you were to wear one of them you'd feel much more confident. Oooh! Strapless!"

"I found something," Isleif said, pulling a pink maribou baby doll nightie from a rack. He fondled the maribou feathers. "This is very goddess-like. It's short, and it will show her breasts well."

"Let me see that," Eirik said, tossing aside a taffeta promlike dress. He groped the maribou, too, for a few seconds before holding the nightie up against himself, smoothing it down this chest. "Yes, this is good. I like it. Do you have bearskin boots? Ones that lace up the thigh?"

"Erm . . ."

"The goddess Fran will need an ax, too," Isleif told her. "A nice little ladies' beheading ax with matching baldric. And a skinning knife to tuck into her boot, for emergencies."

Imogen shoved a periwinkle blue bra into my hands. "Wireless underwire. Truly one of the seven modern miracles of man. Is that a negligee Eirik has? Where did he get it? Oooh, they have it in peach!"

The sales lady made an *eeping* sound, and started backing toward the door. Imogen hurried past Isleif to pounce on the rack of nighties.

"Good point, Isleif," Eirik said, nodding. "She must be protected. Sales slave! I have gold Arabic coins. I will give you two of them for this goddess dress, and one more for the beheading ax and skinning knife."

That turned out to be the straw that broke the sales slave's back. The lady ran for her life as I slumped down into the chair Soren had so quickly vacated, wondering if I was going to go through the rest of my life accompanied by twelve Viking ghosts, clad in a feathery pink nightie.

It was beginning to look like I was.

CHAPTER NINE

"There you are," Ben said, giving me a long look as he stood next to where Imogen had parked her car. "I thought you were going to be back early. Your mother has been looking for you. You only have a few minutes before the Faire opens."

GothFaire is a popular show even though it goes to most places just once a year. People come to it from all around the countryside, which is why we tend to stay parked for a week in smaller towns, sometimes two weeks in big ones. So I wasn't surprised to see that the parking area was already filling even before the Faire was officially open, although it was a bit embarassing having an audience as we all piled out of Imogen's car.

"It looks like a clown car," Mikaela said as she strolled past swinging two chainsaws.

I had to admit, she was probably right. As Isleif, Finnvid, and I tried to squeeze our way out of the back, laden with packages that didn't fit in the trunk of Imogen's car, I just knew the people waiting in line for the ticket booth to open were getting a good show.

"Goddess, you are on my hand—"

"Sorry. Isleif, my shirt is caught on the edge of that bow. Can you—ow! That was my head!"

"Who has the french fries?" Eirik asked, peering out from beneath a mound of packages. The Vikings were not content with their success at the dress shop (although they pouted over the skirt and top I finally picked out, claiming they were lacking in both the feather and breast-presentation departments), and had spent another three hours going to just about every store in Benlös Vessla. We might have been able to stop them after just a couple shops since the shopkeepers didn't take ancient gold coins, but then they spotted a coin dealer who bought precious metals, and all bets were off. "Soren, you are spilling my McShake. If it stains my new silk suit, I will gullet you and hang your intestines to dry in the sun."

"I hear eating," Isleif said behind me. He shifted and the huge hunting bow (with laser sight) smacked me in the head again. "Finnvid is eating our Big Macs!"

"I told you boys, no eating in the car," Imogen said. As the driver, she alone was not laden with packages, but she had been wedged in pretty tightly next to Soren and Eirik. She yanked open the car door behind me, sending me spilling out with my bag containing my date outfit (including a new pair of shoes, nylons, and a froufrou undie set Imogen insisted I have), two bags of men's clothing, a box containing five different flavors of fudge, a Game Boy box and several cartridges, and a cup of Diet Coke. I fell onto the grass with Isleif not far behind me.

"Aha! I knew it! Finnvid is eating our Big Macs!" Isleif shouted as he got to his feet. Finnvid looked guilty with a french fry hanging out of his mouth, but he didn't wait around to explain why he was scarfing down the Vikings' dinner. He threw down all the packages but the seven McDonald's bags, and bolted.

"*Tors vänstra tånagel!*" Eirik erupted from the car, bags and boxes and packages scattering all over the place as he ran after Finnvid. He almost reached him when Finnvid suddenly turned invisible. Eirik shouted again, then did the invisible thing himself. Isleif grunted as he got to his feet, fading away to nothing.

The line of people waiting to get in applauded, evidently believing the Vikings dematerializing was part of the show.

"*Tors* what?" I asked, brushing off myself as I stood.

"*Vänstra tånagel*. It means 'Thor's left toenail.' " Ben handed me one of the bags that had fallen with me.

"Oh. Thanks. You speak Swedish?"

"Yes. You're late," he said again.

"We were delayed by the Vikings," Imogen answered for me, coming around the car with her arms laden (she did as much shopping as the Vikings did—it's a wonder even half of it fit in the car). She kissed Ben on the cheek and hurried off toward her trailer, calling for Soren to bring her things quickly. He limped past me carrying the remains of Imogen's shopping, giving Ben a dark look as he went by.

"So was it Swedish Mr. Laufeyiarson was speaking to you the other night?"

Ben looked surprised for a moment. "Yes, it was. Why?"

"I'm curious why he was talking to you when he knew I was Tesla's owner. What did he say to you?"

It took a few seconds for him to answer. I knew for some reason he didn't want to tell me, but I was less worried about offending him than finding Tesla. "He asked if you were my Beloved. I told him you were. That is all."

"Hmm. You look better," I told him, heading for my trailer. I had just enough time to drop off my things and get my palm reader's clothes on (basically, a gypsy outfit that I'd bought in Hungary).

Ben walked beside me, holding himself stiffly, as if he still hurt. "I told you I would be fine."

"Was that before or after you died?"

"Fran." Ben stopped me, sighing. "I'm sorry I frightened you, but you of all people should know it takes more than a little blood loss to kill me. You overreacted to the situation. Despite appearances, I was not near death."

I shook his arm off and reached for the trailer door. "Oh really? Is that why you didn't answer me when I did the mind thing with you?"

He blinked but said nothing. I gave him a knowing look and ran up the steps to the trailer to change my clothes.

During the summer, GothFaire ran from six at night until two in the morning, which seems like a weird time to run a fair, but given the bizarre nature of the attractions—most popular were the piercing booth (couldn't get me near that with a ten-foot pole), aura photographs, and my mother's potions and spells—the fairgoers liked that we were open so late. I only worked four hours, from the Faire opening until ten. After that I was free, although the rest of the Faire was going full blast.

How is it going? a voice asked me a couple of hours later.

I looked up from the hand I was reading, smiling at Ben standing next to the line of three people waiting to have their palms read. *Are you checking up on me?*

Yes. Do you mind?

I thought about it for a moment as I explained to the man in front of me what his lifeline showed. *That depends. Are you checking up on me to see if I need anything—like a break, or a drink, or something like that—or are you checking up on me just to see what I'm doing?*

The former.

Then I don't mind.

Do you need a break, or a drink, or something like that?

Naw. I only have an hour to go, and things will slow down in a half hour once the magic shows start. What have you been doing?

Are you asking because you are concerned about my well-being, or are you inquiring as to how I've kept myself busy?

I smiled. *I wanted to know if you're all right.*

Ah. I am, thank you. I feel much better. And since I can feel your curiosity, I'll add that I've been sleeping since you and Imogen returned. I woke up a short while ago, and now I'm here to see how I can help you. Do you wish for me to continue hunting for Tesla?

Hmm. I finished the reading for the man before me, smiling when his girlfriend, who was next in line, told me she liked my lace gloves. *I think that's pretty much a lost cause, don't you? We both looked last night, then you looked some before you went all mysterious and almost got yourself killed.*

I think Laufeyiarson has hidden himself and Tesla very well, but if it would make you happy, I will continue to search for them.

No. I don't think searching is going to find them. I spent the next few minutes simultaneously reading a woman's palm, and telling Ben what happened with Tallulah.

Sir Edward didn't say what sort of being the thief was? Ben asked when I was finished.

No. He just said powerful. Tallulah made it sound like bad news. You didn't . . . er . . . you know, kind of know what he was? Because you're a vamp and all?

Ben gave me a look. *Being a Dark One is not synonymous with omnipotence, Fran.*

I love it when you talk with big words. OK, so how do we hunt him down?

I will try to talk to Sir Edward and meet you in an hour, when you are finished.

OK. But I'm going to find Tibolt between shows and

get his help getting rid of the ghosts. I don't think I can go through another day like today.

Ben laughed into my head and did something he'd never done before—kissed me. Mentally. Or rather, he remembered what it felt like for him to kiss me. I gasped as the sensation filled my head of just what he felt when we kissed.

"Are you all right?" the girl in front of me asked as I grabbed a palm-reading flyer and started to fan myself.

"Just a little hot." I made a face at Ben, then turned my attention back to the girl's hand. "Let's see, we were on the Mound of Venus, weren't we?"

An hour later I folded the midnight blue velvet cloth that I used to read people's hands ("Make your space your own," Mom always said), counted out the money, putting it into the GothFaire bag before tucking it away in a lockable metal box I'd picked up in Berlin.

Soren was giving Bruno a last-minute check to make sure the horse's harness was clean. I waved at him as I hurried to drop off the cash box at the trailer. "Have you seen Tibolt?" I asked, stopping for a moment.

He pointed past me. "They just finished their act."

"Thanks!" I popped into the trailer, stashed my money box in its usual place, hurriedly gave Davide some cat food and told him that no, he couldn't go outside when the Faire was open, and hurried out to find Tibolt.

Circus of the Darned people didn't have trailers like the Faire folk. Tibolt had a sleek black RV with a satellite dish clamped onto the top. Ramon and Mikaela had a silver RV, and the three people who worked behind the scenes for them—I never was quite sure of their names since they didn't speak much English—all shared a third RV, much more battered than the other two. I knocked on Tibolt's door, a little surprised when Mikaela answered it.

"Hullo, Fran. Have you come to see Tib?"

"Yes, if he's not busy."

"Sure. Tib? Fran is here for you."

I climbed into the RV, making a mental note that this is what Mom and I needed if we were going to stay with GothFaire. The interior was done in black and red, with gold trim on the black wood paneling. Overhead, a long light hung from the ceiling, while a full couch, two recliners, and a TV made up the living room part. Tibolt was stretched out on the couch, sipping a drink while Ramon sat at the table going over a map of Europe.

"Hi, everyone," I said, feeling a bit out of place in all this opulence. "Tibolt, I came to give you back your pendant, and also to ask if you wouldn't mind using it to get rid of the Vikings. I like them and all, but they pissed off Absinthe this morning, and raised a bit of hell in town, so I think it's best if they were sent to Valhalla."

Tibolt waved his drink at me. "The pendant is yours now. I meant to tell you that earlier, but forgot."

"Mine? I don't think so," I said, pulling the chain over my head. "It's gotten me in enough trouble."

"Regardless, the *Vikingahärta* is dead to me now. It has forsaken me for you."

"Dead?" I looked at the pendant in my hand. It vibrated slightly, as if it was charged with power. "It doesn't feel dead. It's kind of . . . humming."

"Yes. Let me see it." He held out his hand for it. I

plopped it onto his palm. He closed his eyes for a second, then opened them and shook his head, offering me the pendant again. "No, it's as I thought—the *Vikingahärta* has no power for me. It can serve me no purpose now, so you may have it."

"I don't want it!" I said, protesting when he sat up to shove it back into my hands. "It looks valuable and really old. My mom would freak if she found out you gave it to me."

He made a funny little half smile. "Then your mother must understand that in this, we have no choice. The *Vikingahärta* cannot be used by just anyone—the bearer must be sympathetic, open to its abilities. It has chosen you to act through, which is why I said earlier that only you can get send the ghosts to Valhalla. I can do nothing."

"But—I don't have the slightest idea what to do to get them there," I said, my heart sinking. I'd never be rid of the ghosts without help!

"Tib, there has to be something you can do," Mikaela said as he stood and stretched. I narrowed my eyes for a moment, wondering again why the Tibolt magic seemed to have faded. Ever since he'd given me that pendant . . . hmm. Unobtrusively, I set it down on the back of a chair.

"No, and I'm tired of you nagging me about it. Isn't it enough that I'm being unfairly punished by the master?" Tibolt snapped, turning to scowl at me. My knees almost melted at the sight of him—he was gorgeous, so very gorgeous even when he was mad. I wanted to run over and throw myself on him . . . eek! Quickly I grabbed the pendant, sighing in relief when Tibolt's attraction faded into normalness.

Clearly he'd cast some sort of glamour on himself to seem irresistible. I wondered if a bit of that had wonked up my mom's invocation, or if it was the valknut that had thrown her off?

"You're being punished for your own folly," Mikaela said, frowning just as much as her cousin was. "You have no one to blame but yourself for what happened, so blaming Loki or anyone else for your troubles is just denial."

"I know that, you stupid witch!"

Mikaela gasped. Ramon stood up and said, "You will not talk to her that way."

"Don't tell me what to do!" Tibolt yelled as he went toe-to-toe with Ramon. "I'll call her whatever I like!"

"Er," I said, uncomfortable. I had a feeling I was indirectly the source of the argument—or rather, the pendant was—and I would be better off elsewhere. I tried to edge around the two men but they blocked the aisle to the door. "I think I should probably leave now. If you'd let me past . . ."

"You're lucky I am a priestess and not the witch you claim, because if I were, your ass would be so cursed!" Mikaela said, poking Tibolt in the chest and ignoring me just as the other two did.

"You have no powers over me," Tibolt answered, narrowing his eyes at her. "I am a mage of the fifth level."

"And I am the high priestess of Ashtar," she snapped back, giving him another poke in the chest. "Your magic has no effect on me."

"Um, guys? Can I get by, please?" I asked.

"Magic is wasted on the ignorant," Tibolt said as he slammed down his drink and started toward the door. His insult made Mikaela gasp in surprise again.

"Tibolt—" Ramon started to say, but stopped when Tibolt snarled something in Swedish and slammed his way out of the RV.

"I'm sorry," I said quietly, slipping the pendant over my head and scooting past a black-faced Mikaela. "See you guys later."

Mikaela muttered a few things in Swedish, stopping suddenly to call me back. "No, Fran, wait! I will help you with the ghosts."

"You will?" I climbed back into the RV, hesitant because I didn't want to cause any more problems.

"Yes, I will. Tibolt is not the only one in the family with powers, and since he is to blame for the situation, and he refuses to help you, I will." She looked at Ramon, who nodded. "And so will Ramon. We will help you send the ghosts to Valhalla."

"That's awfully nice of you," I said, touching the valknut. "But how are we going to do that?"

"It's very simple," she said, pushing past me to leave the RV. Ramon and I followed. "You know about the Valkyries, yes?"

"Yes," I said, though I was far from an expert on Norse mythology. "Kind of. Ben told me the other night that they're warrior maidens who swoop down on horses and pick out dead warriors to take to heaven, which is called Valhalla."

"Close enough. Queen of the Valkyries is Freya, goddess of love."

"Oh?" I wondered what the goddess of love had to do with dead Vikings.

"Yes. So there's our answer." She ran up the steps to her RV, quickly returning with a tapestry bag. She hurried around the front of the trailer, toward the stretch of woods in which I found Ben. "Come on, we don't have long before our act is on again."

I looked at Ramon. He took my arm and hustled me after Mikaela.

"There's our answer? What answer?" I asked, stumbling over an unseen root. "You don't mean—"

"Yes," Mikaela said, spreading out a cloth and laying out a bowl, candle, and small bouquet of flowers. "We're going to summon Freya and ask her help."

CHAPTER TEN

Crash!

"I was at a party!"

Bang!

"A very nice party!"

Kerwhang!

"In Venice! The city of love! And there were four lovely mortal men practically *drooling* on me with desire!"

Crack. Tinkle, tinkle, tinkle.

I peeked through the fingers I'd slapped over my eyes when Freya, **goddess** of love, warrior queen, and evidently Venetian **party**goer started her hissy fit. The tinkling sound came from the crystal goblet Mikaela had set out as part of the summoning equipment. Freya crushed the goblet between her hands and sprinkled the glass shards on the grass at Mikaela's feet. I had to give Mikaela credit—it took guts to stand up to a really pissed-off goddess (even if she did look like she belonged on the E! channel modeling the latest fashions),

117

but Mikaela didn't budge an inch when Freya got mad at her for being summoned.

"Goddess Freya, I am sorry for disturbing you—"

"And you, you mortal priestess of Ashtar, you think nothing of summoning me from *the* party of the year? Did I mention Elton John was there?"

Mikaela flinched slightly when Freya shredded her invocation cloth. "I'm very sorry, goddess, but this is an emergency."

Freya threw down the cloth, spinning around to glare at Ramon, who stood a few feet away from Mikaela. "You! You are a priest?"

"Yes." Ramon looked like his usual implacable (and silent) self. He didn't even blink when Freya marched over to him.

I was having a hard time wrapping my brain around the idea that first of all, all those Norse gods like Odin and Thor and Freya really existed, and second, that they would look like fashion models. Then again, maybe it was just Freya—beautiful, raven-haired, elegant Freya— who looked like a model. Maybe the rest looked all wispy, and had big beards and wore horned helmets and things.

"Hrmph. Not worth my time." Freya dismissed Ramon and turned to consider me. I thought about clamping my fingers together again so I wouldn't have to see through them, but decided that was too cowardly. Instead I dropped my hands and tried to smile at the irate goddess.

"Hi. I'm Fran," I said politely as she stalked over to me. "I'm not a priestess or anything."

Her eyes narrowed as she examined me from head to

foot. "You are something. You are mortal, but you have been touched by an immortal being."

"Well . . . my boyfriend is a vampire," I told her, praying she didn't call down lightning to smite us, or any of the other godlike things that I'd read about a few years back in a mythology class.

"You are a Beloved? You do not look like a Beloved."

"We're not to that point yet," I said with a kind of cheesey smile. "We haven't even gone on a real date yet, although we're going to do that tomorrow."

She looked interested. "Ah, a first date! I am the goddess of love and romance—you seek my advice, naturally."

"Well—"

"Let me see, a first date . . ." She tapped a finger to her chin while she thought. "Ah, yes! You must seek many lovers."

"Uh . . ." I snapped my mouth shut as soon as I realized it was hanging open. "I must?"

"Yes. As many as you can find. For how else will you know that this Dark One is truly meant to be your soulmate? I made the mistake of marrying young, and without sampling as many men as I could. Luckily, Od left and I was able to see what I was missing, but I would not have you make that same mistake. 'Try before you buy' is one of your mortal sayings, is it not? You must try as many men as you can before you settle for just one."

She looked pleased with herself as I stood in stunned silence, not knowning what I was supposed to say to that. Evidently nothing was expected because she started toward Mikaela, but stopped, looking back at me. "Why do I feel power from you? Nordic power?"

I chewed my lip for a moment before figuring out what was probably bothering her. I pulled the chain around my neck up, displaying the valknut. "Maybe it's from this?"

She hissed and took a couple of steps back. *Vikingahärta!*

"Yeah. Is it bad or something? I raised a group of Viking ghosts with it, which is kind of annoying, but it didn't do anything evil or anything like that."

"It is not bad in itself." She tossed her head and her hair, long, wavy, and black, swung backward to lie in perfection along her silver cocktail dress. The dress itself was studded with crystals (or diamonds—I couldn't tell, although I wouldn't have been surprised to find out they were real diamonds), as were her ankle-strap silver stilettos. "It's the source rather than the pendant itself I would prefer to avoid."

"Fran inadvertantly used the *Vikingahärta* to raise a dozen warriors," Mikaela said carefully. "We desire them to be sent to Valhalla, but are unable to do so. We hoped you would help us."

"Bah," Freya said, using Mikaela's mirrored scrying bowl to check her reflection.

"Er . . . if you don't mind, what is the source of the necklace?" I had to ask the question, although I was a bit worried she'd start breaking things again.

Evidently she'd worked through the worst of her anger, though. She stopped primping in the bowl and tossed it at Mikaela. "That is Loki's valknut. The power comes from him. And because you used it rather than a pendant made in my image, I cannot help you with your warriors."

"But you're the queen of the Valkyries, right?" I asked.

She brushed a speck of something off her dress. "Yes. I am returning to my party now, and if even one of those delicious mortal men who were swooning over me has left, I shall make plain my anger."

"But—but I really do need help with the Vikings," I said, stepping forward to block her as she started to walk past Mikaela. Her eyes widened like she couldn't believe I was obstructing her (she wasn't the only one—my stomach was doing flip-flops at the thought of pissing her off any more). "I understand you can't do anything about the raising of them since it was with this Loki guy's necklace, but you are the queen of the Valkyries, so it seems to me you could help me get them into Valhalla."

"I don't do that sort of thing now," she said, waving a hand at me. A big puff of air suddenly swept up and pushed me aside. "The mortal world offers so much more than the immortal one—television, movies, Hollywood, fashion houses—I spend little time in Valhalla any more. No one there has been on *CSI: Miami*!"

"But—"

"Remember, seek as many lovers as you can find! You will be much happier for that. And you—do not summon me again, priestess," she warned Mikaela, and without another word, she was gone in a suburst of light.

"Oh great. Now what am I going to do?" I asked, plopping down onto a tree stump. "I don't even know this Loki person. Now I have to hit him up for help, too?"

"Loki?" Eirik and a couple of the Vikings emerged from the woods. Eirik was wearing a sleeveless black mesh muscle shirt, and pair of tight leather pants. Gils had on a red T-shirt with the word SEX made up by lizards shaped like letters, and Ljot evidently wanted to go swimming, because he wore a pair of speedos, flipflops, swimming goggles . . . and nothing else. "You are summoning Loki? It is Freya you want. She is the queen of the Valkyries."

I gestured toward Mikaela and Ramon, who were on their knees collecting the debris from Freya's hissy fit. "She was just here. She told us she doesn't go to Valhalla anymore because there are no *CSI* guys there, and that we'd have to ask Loki for help."

"*CSI*?" Ljot asked, adjusting his swim goggles.

"TV show."

"Why did the goddess Freya tell you to summon Loki?" Eirik asked, slapping at a mosquito. I don't know why, but the thought of a ghost with a mosquito bite had me giggling to myself.

"Because this is evidently his. Or was his. Or has his power or something," I answered, standing up to show him the valknut. "So I'll have to try to get him to help, whoever he is."

"You do not know Loki, god of mischief?" Gils asked, disbelief plastered all over his face.

"Nope. I'm not really hip to all the gods. Who is he? And why didn't Freya like him?"

"That would be because of Asgard. Sit, and I will tell you the story of Loki and Freya," Eirik said, making himself comfortable on a fallen log next to me. Ljot and Gils sat on the grass, putting on comfortable "about to hear a story" faces. Mikaela rolled her eyes as she dumped all the debris into a cloth bag, but she and Ramon sat cuddled on her casting blanket to listen.

"Who's Asgard?" I asked, taking my seat again on the tree stump.

"Asgard is a place, not a person. It is where the gods live. Loki was at first a god of much mischief, always pulling jokes on the others, using his powers of transformation to get himself out of trouble. One day, when the gods were constructing Asgard, they found they needed more money to build the wall around it. Loki had the idea of hiring a giant to do the work, and thought up a plan to have the giant work without paying him. He offered the giant the goddess Freya if the wall was completed on time. At first the gods were skeptical, but Loki assured him that he would make sure that the giant did not complete the task on time, so that the gods would not have to pay him for his work."

"What a creep," I said before realizing I was talking about a god. "Er . . . nice creep, of course."

"No, he was not nice," Ljot said grimly, shaking his head.

"The giant had a stallion to help him build the wall. Three days before it was to be finished, the giant was almost done, and the goddess Freya was beside herself with anger at Loki. With the gods behind her, Loki had no choice but to transform himself into a mare, and entice the giant's stallion away. The giant missed the deadline, and was furious. He tried to take Freya anyway, but Thor stopped him. Freya never forgave Loki for using her in such a way."

"Ouch. It was nasty of him to set that up, knowing the giant was going to do all the work and not get paid. I don't blame Freya for being ticked at him." I was about to add that he'd get sued up the ying-yang if he tried something like that now, but remembered in time that we were talking about stuff that happened probably thousands of years ago. Now you see why my brain had such a hard time coping with the fact that all these Norse gods were real people. So much for mythology. "Well, I don't look forward to having to ask him for help, but if there's no other way to get you guys to Valhalla, I'll just have to gird my loins and tighten my belt and grit my teeth, and all that stuff."

I stood up and stretched. Even though it wasn't yet midnight, I was tired.

"We will help you," Eirik said, standing and carefully brushing off the seat of his pants. "Since you will need Loki's goodwill, tonight we will offer a sacrifice in his name to make sure that he views your request for help with favor."

"That would be a nice change," I said, stifling another yawn. "But what sort of sacrifice are you talking about? More mead like Tibolt used?"

"Traditionally we sacrifice a slave," Ljot said, peering through the goggles as if he expected a slave to pop out of the woods and volunteer.

"But you have decreed we not kill anyone," Eirik said

quickly when I turned around to yell at him. "So we will, instead, offer a smaller sacrifice."

"Like what?" I asked, suspicious. "You guys aren't going to kill another rabbit like you did earlier?"

"The rabbit was on the stringy side," Gils said, picking his teeth.

"No, no rabbit. The sacrifice has to be something worthwhile," Eirik said, shooing me toward the trailers. Mikaela and Ramon had already gone off to get ready for their next show.

"What, exactly?" I asked. "You can stop trying to shove me, too. I'm not going anywhere until you tell me what you guys are going to sacrifice."

Eirik sighed and looked up at the stars for a couple of seconds, like he was *so* put upon. "I hope the next goddess who binds us to her is much more reasonable. You need not worry, goddess Fran. We will sacrifice no mortals—only many Big Macs will be offered in the name of Loki."

"And McNuggets," Gils added. "With dipping sauces."

"Yes, McNuggets as well," Eirik said with an "are you happy now?" look on his face.

I smiled. "OK. That sounds fine. Knock yourselves out. I'm a bit tired so I think I'm going to find Ben to say good night, then go to bed early."

"Good night, goddess," they called to me as I headed for the Faire.

"Get the rest of the men together," I heard Eirik say to his men as I left. "Tonight, we pillage McDonald's!"

"I really do not want to know," I said to myself, hurrying so I wouldn't hear them making plans for taking the McNuggets hostage. "It's just better if I don't know."

"What is?"

A man's voice emerged from the dark time-travel booth. Most of the booths, including Desdemona's, had closed during the magic shows.

At least I thought it had closed. "Ben?"

"Oh, Fran!" A light clicked on to show Ben and Desdemona standing much closer than I would have liked. Screw jealousy, Ben was mine! How dare she stand around in a dark booth with him. And how dare he allow her to do it! "I was just showing Benedikt my moonstone. If the moon is in the right quadrant, it casts a light in the darkness. Would you like to see it, too?"

What's wrong? Ben asked, his eyes watching me carefully.

Oh, like you don't know.

"No, thank you," I said politely. "I'm tired. I'm going to bed. Enjoy your moonstone watching, or whatever it is you're doing."

I spun around on my heels, my hands fisted, my jaw tight. And worse of all, my eyes were watering. I was so mad, I didn't know whether I wanted to hit Ben or cry.

Are you going to be jealous every time I'm next to another female?

This is not jealousy. I ran up the steps to my trailer. Thankfully, Mom was still out doing things. *This is righteous indignation, Mister You're-the-Only-Woman-for-Me-I'd-Die-Without-You. You know what I say to that? Bullfrogs!*

Fran, Ben said, sighing into my head. *You are the only*

one for me. I would die without you. And I wasn't doing anything with Desdemona despite her manuevering.

Davide squatted on top of the counter and flattened his ears as I paced up and down the narrow aisle.

Oh, I am so not going to believe . . . wait. You knew she was deliberately luring you into her dark booth?

Ben laughed. *Of course. I'm not an idiot, sweetheart. I know when a woman desires me. But that doesn't mean I feel the same way toward her.*

I thought about that for a minute. Davide's ears straightened up as I stopped to think. *You knew and yet you went anyway?*

I didn't know until I was there.

Oh. There's such a thing as being too passive, though. Did you just stand there while she put her lips all over you? You could have left, you know. You could have said, "No thanks, not interested, and by the way, keep your hands off me or Fran will have a hissy." You could have told her to leave you alone.

You really are silly when you're in the throes of jealousy. I can't decide if it is flattering or annoying.

Annoying? Annoying! Oh! I'll give you annoying, buster!

Davide hunkered down as I stormed past him and yanked open the door to the trailer. I intended to run back out to find Ben so I could punch him in the belly, as he deserved. Instead I stopped as he came up the steps.

"If I were to raise hell every time you spent a few minutes alone with Soren, what would you do?" he asked walking toward me. I took a couple of backward steps past Davide, who was watching us with interest. "If I screamed and yelled and forbade you to spend time with any man, anywhere—your ghosts, Peter, Karl, and Kurt, anyone—would you mind?"

"Soren is a child. He doesn't have the hots for me."

"Like hell he doesn't. His crush on you is evident to everyone." Ben kept walking toward me, his face unexpressive, but his eyes were glowing a rich browny-gold.

"Kurt and Karl are having a fling with Absinthe," I said, backing up another couple of steps.

"Doesn't matter. They could still be attracted to you, and you likewise."

"Peter is old enough to be my dad."

I bumped up against the door that led to the tiny bedroom at the end of the trailer.

Ben put his hands on each side of my head and leaned in, his breath brushing my face in a soft caress. Despite being angry at him, my stomach was twisting and turning happily because he had that look in his eye that he got whenever he kissed me. "How could any mortal man resist such a beautiful, alluring girl as you?"

"I don't care about the mortal ones," I said, my breath coming short and fast as he leaned in even closer. I put my hand on his chest and let his feelings flow into me.

Tell me I'm interested in anyone but you, he commanded, and as an answer, I brushed my lips against his, sliding my arms under his until we were pressed so tightly together, I couldn't tell where I ended and he began.

I might have overreacted a little, I admitted as his tongue flicked over the corner of my mouth. I'd never been one for French kissing before Ben because, I mean—tongues! But it was different with him. It was exciting and wonderful and he tasted like the spicy mulled wine Mom had let me have a sip of last Christmas. My whole body went up in a rush of tingles as I kissed him back, intent on showing him that I appreciated his honesty.

And?

All right, I take your point. I wouldn't like you to be jealous of me being around other guys. So I will try very hard not to care if Desdemona corners you again.

His lips curved against mine in a smile.

But you could tell her hands off, you know! It wouldn't hurt.

He pulled away enough to laugh. "Ah, Fran, you never fail to delight me."

"That's me, good ole entertaining Fran . . . oh. Hi, Mom."

Over Ben's shoulder, my mother's face loomed angry and scowling. He pulled away and half turned to see her.

She tossed down her bag of Wiccan stuff and stood glaring at Ben. "I thought we had an agreement?"

Ben inclined his head slightly. "My apologies. Fran was upset with me, and I was simply trying to straighten things out."

"Agreement?" I asked, licking my lower lip. I could still taste Ben on it, which made my legs feel like they were made of Jell-O. "What agreement?"

"If it happens again, you will leave me no choice," Mom said in a cold voice. She moved aside so the open door could be seen, her arms crossed over her chest.

Ben turned back to me for a moment, caressing my cheek. *Good night, sweet Fran. Sleep well.*

"Hey, wait a sec—Ben! You don't have to leave."

He nodded at my mother, said good night to her, and without another look at me, left the trailer, closing the door behind him.

"What agreement?" I all but yelled, so frustrated I wanted to scream.

"I have told you before that he is not allowed in our trailer," she answered, snatching her bag and brushing past me to get to her room. "I won't have you putting yourself in a dangerous position."

"Dangerous position?" I said, following her to the door to her room. "With Ben? How dangerous can he be? I'm his frickin' Beloved!"

"He's a man," she snapped, whirling around and marching back over to me. "I've seen the way he looks at you, and I will not allow him to use you that way."

My mother has gone insane, I told Ben.

She's concerned for you.

Did she tell you that you couldn't come to our trailer?

We have an agreement, yes. I am allowed to continue seeing you so long as I abide by the boundaries she has set for you.

"You set boundaries for me?" I yelled, so angry I felt like I was going to burst. "I am not a child! You can't treat me like one!"

"You are a minor and my daughter, and I will continue to look out for your interests so long as I need to," she said, slamming her things into a drawer. "Yes, I set boundaries. Someone had to. It was clear to me that you are naive enough, and smitten enough, to allow Ben any liberty."

My mouth hung open for a few seconds. "This is about sex, isn't it? You think I'm going to have sex with Ben? I just barely learned how to kiss him!"

"From what I saw a few minutes ago, you're very well along in your lessons. I will not have you throwing away your life on a . . . a . . ."

"Dark One?" I said, my arms wrapped tight around myself. I was so angry, so hurt that my mother didn't trust me one little bit, my body was shaking, my eyes puddled with tears of frustration.

"Vampire." Mom spat the word out. "He may try to wrap it up in clean linen, but he's a vampire, Fran. Born of the dark powers, he is a parasite on the living, an abomination in the eyes of the goddess."

I grabbed the doorknob. "You can take your goddess and stick her up your—"

"Fran!" Mom shrieked, her face black with anger.

"Ben is not evil. He is not a parasite or an abomination. He's a guy who just happens to be made a little different from most people. And he's my friend. No, he's my *boy*friend. And you can make all the agreements you want with him, but I am not going to honor them. You may not have any trust in me, but I believe in Ben. He'd never hurt me. Never!"

"You foolish, stupid girl," Mom said.

I slammed the door closed, tears running down my face. I thought for a few seconds about running to Imogen's trailer and demanding to stay with them, but I knew my mother would drag me back, and I'd die if anyone saw that. Instead I grabbed my iPod, blanket, and pillow, and curled up on the couch, ignoring my mother when she came out a few minutes later.

CHAPTER ELEVEN

"Good morning, Fran." Imogen stopped on her way past where I was slumped at one of the tables. She looked around the area, then glanced at me, her eyes widenening. "You look horrible."

"That's always so flattering to hear," I said, trying to shake my grumpy mood to give her a smile. It wasn't Imogen's fault my mother was so biased she couldn't understand about Ben and me. "If you're looking for Tibolt, he went off for his run about half an hour ago. Mikaela and Ramon went into town to have something with one of the chainsaws fixed. Peter is off buying supplies for the horses . . . horse."

"I've always felt flattery wasn't needed between friends," she said, setting down her latte and taking a seat opposite me. Imogen wore a pair of white linen shorts, white tank top, and gauzy white and silver blouse over it. "You must have been up early to see everyone about their business."

I eyed the tan leg she swung next to me. "Why is it

that female Moravians can get a tan, but the men can't tolerate the sunlight?"

"It has something to do with the nature of the original curse, I believe," Imogen said, shrugging slightly as she sipped her latte. "Now, are you going to tell my why you look so horrid this morning, or shall I have to guess?"

"Mom and I had a fight over Ben."

"Ah," she said, nodding.

I flicked a piece of orange peel from my breakfast into the nearby trash. "You're not surprised?"

"That your mother is threatened by Benedikt? No. She would not be a loving parent if she wasn't concerned for you."

"Oh, not you too," I said, rubbing my forehead. "I'm sixteen, I'm not a child! I don't need someone watching out for me. I'm perfectly able to take care of myself. I'm a Beloved, for heaven's sake!"

"No, Fran, you're not," she said, setting down her cup and taking my hand in hers. I'd only recently started allowing Imogen to touch my hands. She had a lot of emotions that I didn't think were any of my business, but I knew she loved Ben, and like me a lot, so I didn't flinch when she took my hand, giving it a little squeeze. "You were born to be his Beloved, yes. But you have not yet completed the seven steps to Joining with him, and until you do that, you cannot comprehend what it is to bind yourself to one man for an eternity. You cannot imagine what you will be sacrificing in order to be his Beloved. Your mother understands some of that, and she's just trying to protect you as best she can."

I made a face. "I doubt it. She's just being a control

freak and trying to keep me under her thumb. She still thinks I'm a little kid, and I'm not!"

"Of course you're not. You have great powers, but more importantly—" Imogen drew a ward over my chest—"you have a large, caring heart. You put other people before yourself, and no child would do that. But you do have to give your mother a little credit for wanting to keep you from being hurt. She has seen more of the world than you have."

"I know." I sighed, my anger melting slightly. "Although she hasn't raised a herd of Vikings, or killed a demon. And she's not dating a vampire."

Imogen smiled. "I have an uncle she might like—but that's neither here nor there. Now, other than your fight with Miranda, what are you looking so very blue about?"

"Oh . . . everything." I flicked the last bit of orange skin into the trash. "The date tonight. The Vikings I can't seem to send home. Tesla missing, and me helpless to find him. Ben keeping secrets from me."

"Very well. I was going to have a swim with Tibolt today, but you need my help far more than he needs to pay attention to me." Imogen set her cup down.

I giggled at the way she phrased her plans for Tibolt.

"Let us take this step by step. Your date tonight with Benedikt—your mother has not forbidden you to go out with him?"

"No. And she'd better not," I said, thinning my lips.

"Good. Your outfit you have taken care of. That just leaves the setting, and that's up to Benedikt. I have given you valuable advice on how to act, so I don't see that you have any worries where the date itself is concerned."

"Well . . . I'm a bit worried about the Vikings."

"Why?" Imogen asked. "I haven't seen them attack anyone lately."

Timing is everything. At that moment Isleif strolled by, wearing a pair of scarlet-and-orange striped biking pants and purple tank top. In one hand he had his hunting bow, the other a book of dog breeds. "Good morning goddess, Imogen. I'm going hunting for poodles. Would you like to join me? I hope to get enough to make a pair of poodle fur leggings."

I looked at Imogen.

She sighed.

"If we run across a herd of them, I should have enough pelts to make you a pair as well," Isleif generously offered.

"Are there any poodles on the island?" I asked Imogen under my breath.

"Not that I've seen. No one lives here but the archeaology people, and they only have golden retrievers."

"Knock yourself out," I said to Isleif. He stared in surprise. "Um. I mean, go right ahead. Have fun. Happy . . . er . . . poodling."

"Very well," Imogen said as he walked away. "I concede that the Vikings are an issue, although I'd like to point out that Finnvid has not been any trouble, and has a most delicious way with . . . but that's beside the point."

"Not to mention way too much information." I smiled.

"Next on your list is Tesla, and I believe you and Benedikt have done all you can there. I wish there was something I know of to help, but short of hiring a detective to investigate—something that would be bound to cost a great deal of money—I'm at a loss."

I rubbed my forehead again. The headache I thought I'd gotten rid of this morning was back. "Yeah, me too."

"And as for Benedikt keeping secrets—you must realize, Fran, that he has commitments to people other than yourself."

"I know that. He told me about his blood brother. Or rather, he told me that he couldn't tell me about him. Something about an oath. Which I understand, I really do. But it's still kind of annoying to have him disappear for a month and pop back up and not say where he's been. Or go off for the night and come back almost dead!"

"I admit that last annoyed me, as well," she agreed. "But you must learn to trust Benedikt. He would never do anything that would harm you."

"I know that. I just hate that he's off doing probably really neat things without me."

She smiled. "I sense that your feelings for him are becoming deeper than perhaps you realize."

"Not going there," I said, sighing again. Sometimes life seemed so overwhelming.

"All right, we won't. Out of your four issues, I believe only one is a legitimate concern, and I can help you with that."

"With the Vikings?" I stopped rubbing my forehead to squint into the morning sun that shown over her shoulders.

"Yes. You wish to send them to Valhalla, correct?"

"Yeah." I told her what had happened the night before. "I was going to summon this Loki god guy, but

Mikaela went off to get a chainsaw fixed, so I'm stuck waiting until they get back."

"Nonsense," Imogen said, drinking the last of her latte and throwing the paper cup into the trash. She stood, dusting herself off. "You have me."

"I do?" I got up slowly, not sure what she was getting at.

"Yes, you do. I shall summon the god Loki, and you will lay your case before him."

"But . . . you're not a witch. Or a priestess, for that matter."

"No, I'm Moravian. That is infinitely better," she said without the slightest trace of arrogance. I followed her to her trailer, and waited while she dug out a book of invocations and grabbed a few odd items from one of the drawers under her couch. I glanced a couple of times at the door to her bedroom, knowing Ben must be in there since he usually slept through the early part of the day, when the sun was at its strongest.

"Shall we?"

I nodded and trotted obediently at her heels as we made our way through the just-waking-up fair to a small sandy area that jutted out of a rocky stretch of beach.

"This is a nice quiet place where we shouldn't be disturbed," she said, nodding at me to set my armload down. I helped her spread out a blanket, pour a little water into a metal chalice, and lay out some flowers, a big black feather, and a large curved animal claw.

"Have you done this much?" I asked, chewing my lip a little as she consulted her book.

"Not with Norse gods, no. But it can't be that hard if

Mikaela did it. Now, let's see . . . for the earth we have pu-
rified water and—just grab a handful of dirt would you?
Set it in that little cup. Perfect. Nature is represented by
the flowers, and the animal kingdom by the feather and
bear claw. Hmm." She looked up, her lips pursed. "It says
to summon a god we must first be in a religion that hon-
ors the god, or possess a personal talisman of the god
himself. Did Freya say that amulet belonged to Loki?"

I shook my head. "She just said it had his power in it."

She looked thoughtful for a second or two before closing the book. "That sounds good enough to me. You'll
have to do the invocation since the amulet is yours."

"Um . . . I don't know what invocation to use for
him."

She flipped through the book for a few minutes before closing it again. "I believe we just make something
up. So long as it's about Loki, asking for his help, and using the amulet to reach him, it should be all right."

"OK. I'm not very good at this, but anything is worth a
shot to get the Vikings on their way."

"I'll help. How do invocations usually start?"

I thought for a minute, then knelt behind the arrangement of elements that we'd laid out. "By leaf and flower,
by water and earth, by feather and claw, I do invoke
thee, Loki."

"Oh, that's very nice," Imogen said, looking impressed.

"Thanks. I do sometimes listen to my mother."

She smiled at my grin, then looked serious. "How
about this next—'shape changer, sky traveler, god of fire
riding in the sky; descend upon your daughters, we be-
seech thee.' "

"Wow. You're good," I said, then repeated the words to make sure I remembered them. The valknut started glowing hot under my shirt. I pulled it out, showing it to Imogen.

"Oooh, it's glowing! That must mean it's working."

"I hope. Let's see . . . 'aid me in my time of need, oh Loki whose power moves the universe.' "

"Appealing to his vanity—excellent choice," Imogen said, nodding.

"Um . . . what next? I'm drawing a blank."

"Oh, let me. I know a little something about Norse mythology. I must know something about Loki that we can use . . . hmm. Let's try this: 'Loki Laufeyiarson, full of fire, strong in spirit, searing all with your splendor, grant me your presence!' Then repeat the first part again."

"Eh . . . did you say Laufeyiarson?" I asked, wondering if that was a common name.

"Yes. Loki is the son of Farbauti and Laufrey, if I remember my mythology correct. Why?"

"It's just that I know someone with that name . . . naw. It's got to be a coincidence. OK, here I go. Let's hope this works."

I spent a few moments clearing my mind of extraneous thoughts, took a couple of deep breaths as I got a firm grip on the valknut, mentally spelled out the word Loki in my head to use as a focusing image, and then spoke the full invocation.

". . . by leaf and flower, water and earth, feather and claw, I invoke thee now!" I finished, staring at my hand where the valknut suddenly burst forth with blinding light.

"Imogen?" I asked, trying to shade my eyes against the bright light. It was like staring into one of those huge arc lights they use for movie premieres—or so I imagined, never having been idiot enough to do that. "Are you OK?"

"Yes. Did it work? I can't see anything."

"I think it's fading," I said squinting. The light in the center of the starburst changed, turning black as a man's shape formed and turned into a person.

"Who summons me?" the furious voice of a man asked. I still had sunspots in my eyes, but as I blinked them away, I got a good look at the god we'd summoned.

"You!" I yelled, gritting my teeth. "I want my horse back!"

The red-haired man who'd offered me a thousand bucks for Tesla looked startled for a moment, his eyes quickly narrowing. "I don't know what you're talking about."

"Yes, you do," I snarled, marching up to him, shaking my fist at him. "I want Tesla back! Don't you dare deny you took him, because you're the only one who has been interested in him. Now, where is he? What did you do to him? Is he all right? Is he getting enough to eat? I swear by all that's holy, if you've hurt him, I'm going to kick you in the happy sacks so hard, you won't be able to walk for a week!"

"Fran!" Imogen shrieked, running to stand next to me, pulling down the fist I was waving under Mr. Laufeyiarson's nose. "One does not threaten to kick a god, let alone to emasculate him. I take it you know Loki?"

"I have never met this deranged, violent young woman before," Loki Laufeyiarson lied. He didn't seem to be overly concerned about my threats, either, but I didn't let that stop me.

"Oh, I know him. He offered me a thousand bucks for Tesla, and when I wouldn't sell him, he stole poor Tesla! You may be a god, but you just can't go around stealing other people's horses!"

Loki pulled himself up until he was several inches taller than me. I wondered for a moment how he did that, then remembered—Norse god. Probably growing a couple of inches was no big deal to him. "I am one of the Elders, mortal. I can do whatever I desire."

"Yeah? Well, maybe I should just call Freya back. I bet she'd have something to say about that. And maybe that Odin guy, too. Isn't he supposed to be the head god?"

A little something flashed in his brown eyes, something like worry. I smiled to myself, happy I'd found a pressure point.

"All right," he said, kind of grinding his teeth as he spoke. "Since you summoned me for this purpose, I will put your mind at rest and admit I took the horse you call Tesla. But I had a very good reason for doing so."

"Yeah? What would that be?" I asked, worried he was going to say he used to own Tesla. One of the problems of getting a horse without its history is that you never quite know just who owned him over the years.

"He is an offspring of mine."

Chapter Twelve

I goggled. I just opened my mouth and let my eyes bug out in a good old-fashioned goggle. "He *what?*" Loki was clearly insane.

"He is the descendant of Sleipnir, the eight-legged horse I bore and gave to Odin. Only a few horses exist today that can trace their heritage back to me—the white stallion Tesla is one of them."

"OK, OK, time out here," I said, freaking out a bit. "You're a god, a male god, and you gave birth to an eight-legged horse? Wait! This wouldn't have been when you were trying to make some giant mess up his work schedule with Asgard?"

Loki looked down his nose at me. "The events at Asgard have been skewed out of proportion, but yes, it is while I was in the form of a mare that I became pregnant with Sleipnir. Now you see why the white stallion is valuable to me."

"To be frank, no. I mean, the whole thing about you changing yourself into an animal and giving birth aside,

Tesla has to be . . . what a couple of hundred generations away from Sleipnir?"

Loki waved away that point. "The fact remains he is an offspring, and I have precious few of them left these days."

"Yeah, but . . . you're Loki. God of mischief, the trickster. You do all sorts of mean things to other gods. It's a little hard to believe that all of a sudden you've turned into a family guy."

He shrugged. "People change with time. So have I."

"You're a god," I pointed out yet again in case he'd forgotten that point, or thought I was so stupid I had.

"And who is to say gods cannot have a change of heart?" he asked, one eyebrow going up in question.

He had a point there.

"Tesla is just an old horse. He needs to be taken care of. He doesn't need some—" I bit off the phrase "deranged old man who thinks he's a god" and replaced it with, "—one who is busy with other things. Besides, I promised I'd take care of him, and I don't go back on my promises."

"I believe the phrase 'too bad, so sad' comes to mind," he answered, examining his fingernail like he needed a manicure. "Tesla is mine now."

"Oh, you . . . gah!" I yelled.

"You're being terribly inconsiderate of Fran," Imogen said. She had on what I thought of as her haughty face, the one she used with guys who got rude with her. "All she's doing is trying to get her horse back, and help some ghosts to move on to Valhalla. She has a very important first date with my brother tonight, and because you're being obstinate and obstructive, she's not going to enjoy it as she should because she'll be worrying about Tesla, and what the ghosts are doing while she's on the date."

"A date?" Loki asked, looking from Imogen to me. "You have a date with a Moravian?"

"Yes, Ben's a Dark One, but that isn't really important—"

"A Beloved on her first date," Loki interrupting, stroking his chin as he gave me a speculative look. I groaned to myself. I knew that look. I knew what was coming next. "How well I remember the courtships of all three of my wives. I will give you some valuable advice."

"I have already advised Fran as to the best way to enjoy her date," Imogen pointed out. "Input by a man is hardly necessary."

"First, you test this Dark One to see if he's really faithful to you," Loki said, totally ignoring Imogen. "I recommend playing a trick or two on him to see if his heart is true, or if he's a lying dog."

"My brother does not lie!" Imogen said, outraged.

"Next, take something away from him that he values greatly. When the time is right, pretend you found it, and he will be grateful to you forever."

"Oh!" Imogen gasped. "That is completely out of line! Fran, don't you listen to a word this man is saying!"

Loki continued to ignore her. I just hoped the advice would end soon, so I could get back to the topics of Tesla and the Vikings. "Finally, you must bring him many gifts. Something to give you value in his eyes, and make him cherish you as the source of great fortune."

I couldn't help but roll my eyes at his advice. I may be naive where dating is concerned, but even I knew what he was recommending was downright stupid.

"You need some serious psychological counseling," Imogen told him with a sniff.

"I am finished," Loki told me. "Now that I have given you the gift of my advice, you may thank me and then I will leave."

"Thank you for the advice." No matter how awful it was. "But I'm not quite through talking to you about Tesla and the Vikings."

"I've told you my answer," he said, starting to walk away. "There is nothing left to discuss."

Just in time I remembered that I wasn't as powerless as he thought. I whipped the amulet out and held it up so the sunlight glinted off it. "Recognize this?"

His eyes widened as he took a step toward me, his hand outstretched. "The *Vikingahärta!* What are you doing with it? It is mine!"

"Nuh uh." I held the valknut close to my chest and gave him a victorious smile. " 'Too bad, so sad,' remember? The *Vikingahärta* is mine now."

"Fran," Imogen hissed between her teeth as she came to stand next to me. "It is not wise to tease a god!"

Loki said something in a language I didn't understand, but the mean tone of his voice was enough to tell me he wasn't offering up a prayer for my good health.

"Don't worry, I'm in control," I whispered to Imogen before turning back to Loki with a pleasant smile. "However, I'm willing to let you have it if you give me back Tesla, and send the Viking ghosts I raised with it to Valhalla."

"No," Loki said, and took another step toward me.

"No? Like . . . no?" The *Vikingahärta* glowed warm in my hand, but whether it was heating up because I was suddenly starting to sweat, or if it was warming of its own power, I didn't know.

"No. No, I will not release my descendant into your custody, and, no, I will not help you with any warriors. You will give the *Vikingahärta* to me now, or you will suffer the consequences."

"That would not be fair to Fran," Imogen said, her chin held high. "You would take everything from her and give her nothing in return. I cannot allow you to do that."

"You cannot *allow* me?" Loki said, his voice suddenly getting very deep and very big. So big it echoed off the rocks behind us, scaring the seagulls above into silence. "You would threaten me, immortal?"

Imogen gave him a look I'd seen bring other men to their knees. "I would protect my friend's best interests from a greedy god, yes."

"Bah!" Loki waved a hand at Imogen. Without a sound, she fell over backward onto the sand, narrowly missing hitting her head on a large chunk of driftwood.

"Imogen!" I screamed, falling to my knees next to her to see how badly she was hurt. I felt for a pulse, and was relieved to feel it beating away strong and steady. Her eyes were closed, her face peaceful, but it was as if she'd fallen asleep standing there. "What did you do to her?" I asked, looking up at Loki, ready to call for backup help if he'd harmed her.

"Merely stopped her squawking for a few minutes.

147

She is immortal. She is not harmed, merely sent to sleep."

"If she doesn't wake up in a minute, you're going to be one very sorry god," I promised, slowly getting to my feet.

He sighed, his eyes hard and glinting with anger. "More threats. Very well, I have one for you, mortal. If you do not return to me the *Vikingahärta*, I will take that which you most value."

Cold gripped my heart, a number of images chasing each other through my mind—Ben, my mother and father, Tesla, Soren and Imogen . . . I valued all of them highly. "Take? Take them where?"

The look he gave me made the cold in my heart turn to ice.

"Give me the valknut now, mortal Fran." The voice coming out of his mouth seemed to be amplified, as if he was speaking through a bullhorn. It was so loud, it hurt my ears.

I took a couple of steps backward, shaking my head slowly, the pendant clutched tight in my hand. "Not unless you give me back Tesla, and take the Viking ghosts to Valhalla."

His eyes narrowed. "You would sacrifice that whom you hold most dear for one small, insignificant piece of jewelry?"

"No, I would not." I glanced quickly at Imogen, but her chest rose and fell normally, so I figured Loki was telling the truth and she was just asleep. "I would, however, fight with every last breath in my body for them. If you want this valknut, you're either going to have to take it from me, or give me what I want."

Loki snarled something under his breath and lunged for me, but the valknut, despite being his and seeped in his power, evidently didn't like him much, for it suddenly blasted out a reddish gold light that had Loki leaping backward.

"Very well," he growled, his body starting to shimmer. "We shall do things the hard way."

He shimmered off into nothingness before I could say anything. One second he was there, the next he was gone, just a few sparkly bits in the air left to indicate that a god had been standing there.

Imogen moaned.

"You OK?" I asked her, kneeling next to her. "How do you feel?"

She rubbed her head. "Like someone struck me. What happened? Ew. I'm lying on seaweed."

I brushed her off and helped her pick seaweed from her long silver blond hair, explaining what Loki had done and said.

"Oh! He is not going to get away with treating us this way," she said, her eyes fired with anger. "Just wait until Benedikt hears about this!"

"Um. Yeah." A chill rippled down my arms at the memory of Loki swearing he would take whoever mattered the most to me. "Maybe we shouldn't tell him about this."

"Not tell him?" Imogen paused in the middle of gathering up her Loki invocation things. "Fran, you cannot keep secret from Benedikt something of this importance."

"Why not, he doesn't seem to have any problem in keeping secrets from me." I handed her the chalice.

She dumped the water from it and frowned at me. "That's different, and you know it."

I didn't see the difference, actually, but an argument about that wasn't going to do either of us any good at that moment. I stayed silent as we walked slowly back to the trailers, Imogen lecturing me the entire time about having confidence in Ben.

"Fran!" Imogen said as she stopped next to the steps to her trailer. I handed her the things I'd picked up. "You haven't listened to a thing I've been saying, have you?"

"Actually, I have."

She opened the door to her trailer, glanced inside to make sure Ben wasn't up and about, tossing the things onto the seat nearest the door. "You can't just do nothing about this! Ignoring it won't make it go away."

"Oh, I know that. And I'm not going to do nothing."

"What are you doing, then?" she asked.

Finnvid and Gils were laying out on the chaises in the center area, a boombox between them, getting a tan while listening to music and swigging back what looked like a case of Swedish beer.

"I'm going to ask Sir Edward for help. Now that I know who I'm up against, I just need to figure out a way to make Loki do what I want."

"Loki?" Finnvid asked, looking up from a magazine with topless women all over its pages. "Did you summon him? Did he like the sacrifice of many small hamburgers we made in his name? Will he help us get to Valhalla?"

"Yes, I have no idea, and no. He's being really annoying, and I'm going to have to get tough with him," I said as I marched past the two ghosts.

150

"Gils, wake up," Finnvid said, smacking his friend on the head with the magazine. "The goddess Fran is going to war against Loki. We must help her!"

"No, it's not a war—"

"*Idag dör vi!*" Finnvid shouted at the top of his lungs. "*Nästa hållpats: Valhall!*"

"Shhhh!" I hissed, clapping a hand over his mouth. "Some people sleep in late! And what did you say?"

"Today we die. Next stop: Valhalla," Finnvid said from beneath my hand. I pulled it back to let him speak since he wasn't bellowing anymore. "Ah, see? The others come."

"Oh, great, just what I . . . no, no, put down the bow, Isleif."

"Finnvid called us," Isleif said, puffing a little since he had run up from the shore. Behind him were Ref and Ljot, with Eirik emerging at a full gallop from the woods, tucking his shirt into his leather pants. "We go to battle?"

"No! No battle!"

"Yes!" Finnvid said, waving his arm at the other Viking ghosts as they materialized and emerged from various parts of the island, all attracted by his war cry. "The goddess Fran goes to war against Loki! It will be a battle like none other!"

"You can say that again," I muttered under my breath.

CHAPTER THIRTEEN

"First, we must draw Loki into an area where he is unprotected," Eirik said, shaking a ballpoint pen that wouldn't write. He made an annoyed sound and threw it down along with the tablet of paper he'd taken from my trailer. "Gils, do you have your laptop?"

"Yes, right here," Gils said, hauling out a small white laptop. He sat down with it at one of the picnic tables. The rest of the Vikings clustered around him to watch over his shoulder.

"You guys bought a laptop yesterday?" I asked, having a bit of a problem trying to cope with the thought of one-thousand-year-old ghosts with computers.

"Two. Mine is getting a memory upgrade and a Firewire card, and should be ready later today," Eirik answered as Gils booted up a graphics program. He directed him to draw a rough map of the area. "We need a nice spot to ambush him. How about behind the main tent, where the Wiccans hold their circle? It is enclosed on three sides."

"Look, I really appreciate everyone thinking they have to help me, but you know, it's probably going to be easier for me to do it myself," I told them, but no one paid the least bit of attention to me.

"The goddess Fran can draw him into the area tonight, when the sun is at its lowest, so Loki's power will be at its ebb," Isleif explained. "Then when he is in position, we will strike."

"I will cut off his head," Gils said.

"And I will cut out his spleen." Ljot brandished a hunting knife with great pleasure.

Isleif's eyes lit up. "I will shoot him full of arrows that will pierce every major organ."

"That's a really sweet thought, guys," I said, trying again to make them see reason. "But this is a god we're talking about, remember? I know the twelve of you are big and bad Vikings, but Tallulah's boyfriend Sir Edward said that Loki was like nothing he'd seen before, and he had a whole lot of power. So I don't think you guys are going to be able to defeat him even if you do ambush him."

"The goddess Fran has a point," Finnvid said thoughtfully, looking at Eirik.

"Hmm. Perhaps she does. Loki still has much power. It couldn't hurt to have some help. Very well—Thorir, you and Ref summon the Vangarians."

"The who?" I asked.

"Vikings, of a sort. They sailed primarily into Russia," Eirik explained. "We used to war with them, but they will join us in a battle against Loki. Tonight, when the sun is at its lowest, the goddess Fran will drawn Loki into our trap, and we will spring it on him, killing him once and for all."

The others made happy noises of agreement. I wanted to whap them all on the head with a lady's small beheading ax. "Sheesh! What part of 'he's a god' do you not understand? You can't kill him! And even if you could, I don't want him dead—I just want him to give me back Tesla, and to send you all on your way."

Instantly twelve Viking faces turned pouty.

"Oh, for heaven's sake . . . look, even if I agreed to this plan—and I'm not!—I couldn't help. I've got a date with Ben tonight, remember?"

"The big date," Gils said, pursing his lips. "The goddess should not miss that."

Isleif nodded. "It is important."

Eirik paced back and forth for a few seconds. "Very well. We will use some other bait than the goddess to ensnare the god Loki. Then when we have him—"

"I will cut out his liver, cook it before him, and make him eat it while it's still smoking," said an enthusiastic Ljot.

"No liver cutting!" I yelled.

"Then we will hold him prisoner until the goddess is done with her date and can force him to her will," Eirik said, shaking his head at Ljot. I could have sworn I heard him muttering something to Ljot about how later they would cut out Loki's liver, but it could have been my paranoid imagination.

"Whatever. Just so there's no killing, no liver cooking, and no messing with anyone in GothFaire. If I hear one more complaint from Absinthe about you guys . . ."

I shot them all meaningful looks. They all, every single one of them, tried very hard to look innocent.

"We haven't raped, pillaged, plundered, or murdered anyone in days," Finnvid grumbled. "Well . . . we did pillage the McDonald's last night for the sacrifice."

"And see how much good that did," I answered, making a mental note to find out if they had left any money for the hamburger sacrifices.

"You will go now, goddess, and get ready for your date," Eirik said, shooing me away when I tried to see what Gils was busily typing in on his laptop. Just when did he learn to use one? Not to mention learn to type? "We will take care of everything here."

"That's just what I'm afraid of."

"We will summon the Vangarians to help us catch the god Loki. We will not kill anyone. We will wait for you to come back from your date before torturing him. You see? All is in hand. Go have your date."

I glanced at the sun's position in the sky. "I have about five hours before I have to get ready for my date. Why don't I help you guys, instead?"

"You are a goddess!" Eirik said in a voice filled with fake shock. He grabbed my elbow and hustled me off in the opposite direction from Gils and his laptop. "We would never ask you to work. That would be wrong."

"Uh huh." I let myself be manuevered, but only because I didn't think there was much the Vikings could do to screw things up so long as they promised no one would be killed and flame-roasted.

"We'll see you later, when the trap is ready for the god Loki." Eirik released my arm and gave me a gentle shove.

I stopped and let him have a bit of a glare. "Fine. But stay out of trouble! I'm going to talk to Sir Edward while you guys are making your big plans. Just remember! No killing! No maiming! No general destruction."

"Be on your way, goddess," Eirik said with one last shove. "We have work to do."

I had work too, but I put that thought aside as I trotted over to Tallulah's trailer. I figured it was much more important to talk to Sir Edward about what he knew about Norse gods than cleaning the trailer.

My mother had other ideas.

What are you doing?

Cleaning the bathroom in our trailer. Mom caught me as I was leaving Tallulah's. *How are you feeling?*

As good as ever. What were you talking to Tallulah about?

I was talking mostly to Sir Edward about Norse gods. I gave the shower wall one last wipe with the sponge, and called it good, tossing the cleaning things into a bucket we kept in the cupboard under the sink.

Ah. Imogen told me what happened between you and Loki this morning. You should have called for me. I don't like the idea of you two standing up to a god.

I snorted as I glanced outside. The Vikings had long since disappeared. They were gone when Mom found me and dragged me in for some forced cleaning. I figured they were out calling up all their ghost friends to help them with Loki. *Right. First of all, it was early morning and you were asleep.*

Fran, you can wake me up if you need me.

I know that. But we didn't need you. We were in control of everything.

It was Ben's turn to snort. *That's why Imogen was struck with a sleeping spell?*

She wasn't hurt. I would have called you if she had been hurt.

Nonetheless—

Sir Edward said the only way to get a god to comply with your desires is to use his power against him, I said, interrupting what was sure to be yet another macho guy lecture.

You're changing the subject. Irritation seeped into my head with the words.

I giggled and started on the tiny kitchen area of the trailer. With just a couple of counters, a miniscule stove, and tiny sink, it wouldn't take me long to clean it up. *Yep. Do you think the valknut is going to be power enough to use against him?*

Ben was silent for a moment. *I will see that it is.*

I frowned as I wrung out the washrag. *Is something wrong? You sound distracted. What are you doing?*

Taking a shower.

Oh! For some bizarre reason, a little tiny blush warmed my cheeks. *Right this second?*

Yes. Why? Don't you believe me?

Sure. I just . . . it's kind of odd talking to someone while they're naked and soapy.

His slow smile stole across my mind. *Would you like me to prove it?*

Prove it? What do you mean?

Sensation flooded my head, the feeling of Ben

stroking his hands down his wet, soapy chest, his long fingers leaving a trail as they slid down his breastbone to his belly. The image was so strong, so clear in my mind, my own fingertips tingled as if it was my hands touching him.

Oh man. You're . . . oooh.

I was thinking about kissing you a few seconds ago. Now I'm imagining it's you touching me. His fingers spread out over his belly. The combination of what he was thinking and feeling made my own stomach turn over in excitement. *But what I'd really like is for you to touch me here.*

His hands slid lower, the soap turning his skin into wet, slippery silk. I gasped, my eyes almost bugging out when he started washing his guy parts. OK, I'm no idiot, I knew he had those parts. I knew what they were and all, having had to sit through a couple of years of sex ed and things like that, and didn't think they were that big a deal. And although I was secretly interested in knowing what Ben—all of Ben—looked like, I wasn't ready for *him* to know that I wanted to know.

Is this too much for you? he asked as he soaped himself up. *If you want me to, I'll stop.*

Well . . . you have to get the soap off, so I don't think you can stop right now, I said, my mouth hanging open as I stood there trying not to let him see how interested I was.

I meant I'd stop sharing myself with you. His voice was warm in my head, reassuring, and yet stirring something deep inside me.

My mother entered the trailer, Davide at her heels. "Done already? That didn't take you long."

Just because I don't want to have sex with you doesn't mean I'm not . . . um . . .

Curious?

Yeah.

"Fran? Are you all right? You have an odd expression on your face."

The sensations of warm water that cascaded down his body were as vivid in my mind as his. *There are some things I cannot share with you, Fran. But everything else I have is yours, including my body. Whenever you're ready for it.*

"Honey? What's wrong?"

I blinked a couple of times to get rid of the vision of a wet, naked Ben. My mother stood directly in front of me, staring. "Are you all right? You're panting. If you don't close your mouth, you're going to catch flies."

"Yeah. I was just . . . uh . . . thinking of something."

"Hmm." She gave me a suspicious look, but moved past me. "Why don't you put those things away. I want to have a talk with you."

I put the last of the cleaning things away, and sat down on the couch while she unloaded her invocation items. She chatted about how the day's circle had gone, just the same old stuff I'd heard a hundred times. I mentally turned down her voice a couple of notches.

How about in two hours? I asked Ben, trying for a light, playful tone, but I suspected he knew I was reeling in my tongue and drying not to drool.

For our date, you mean?

Yeah. Not anything else. I'm not ready for that yet.

I know, sweetheart. And you know that I will not rush you. I've waited more than two hundred years for you. I can wait a few more until you are comfortable with the thought of physical intimacy.

I'd never talked like this with anyone before, and I had an odd feeling I should be embarassed to be talking about sex, not to mention more or less watching Ben take a shower, but I wasn't. Ben was different from every other person, and not just because he was a vampire. He was . . . right.

Thank you.

Huh?

I think you're the right person for me, too.

Stop eavesdropping! I yelled, mortified.

He laughed. *I wasn't. You're projecting to me. If you don't want me to hear your thoughts, you'll have to shield them.*

Oh great, now I'm a radio station. Well, WFRAN is going off the air now. I'll see you in a bit.

"Fran? What is wrong with you today?"

I dragged my mind back from Ben and realized that once again my mom was standing in front of me, having evidently been waiting for me to answer a question I didn't hear. "Sorry. Just thinking about things."

Her lips thinned. "It's Ben, isn't it? You were thinking about him."

I decided what could work for Ben could work for me. I said nothing, just looked at my mother.

Her lips thinned even more. I swore to myself that no matter how much she ragged on Ben or me, I wasn't going to get into another knockdown, drag-out with her.

Things between us had been strained and tense since the last fight, and although I knew she was wrong about Ben, I didn't see that there was going to be any way of convincing her of that. She'd just have to see for herself what a trustworthy guy he was.

"Very well," she said, sitting down on the opposite side of the little table. "Now is as good a time as any to discuss this date you have with him tonight."

I continued to say nothing. I sure thought a whole lot of things, though. I thought so many, and thought them with so much mental hand waving and general freaking, I had to double-check first to make sure that I wasn't broadcasting to Ben.

Mom took a deep breath and let it out slowly. "I'm not going to say I'm sorry about the argument we had the other night, primarily because I don't believe I have to apologize for caring about my daughter and worrying about her health and safety, but also because I can see by the sullen look on your face that it wouldn't do any good."

I fought down the urge to touch my face. Sullen? Me? I wasn't feeling sullen. Tired, yes; wary, oh yes. But sullen? Nope. Not this girl.

"However, I believe one good thing came out of that ugly scene—I know now the depths of your feelings for Benedikt."

It was on the tip of my tongue to tell her that I didn't think she did, because not even I knew how I felt for Ben, not in the way she meant, at least. My feelings for him were still confused and more or less up in the air. Oh, I liked him. I liked how he shared himself in the shower. I *really* like kissing him. But anything beyond that was still unknown territory.

"As for your accusation that I don't trust you—" Mom paused a minute and frowned at me.

So much for not talking about the fight.

"—I want you to know that I do trust you. If I didn't, I wouldn't allow you to go on this date."

My back straightened up at that "allow" business, but I decided to let it go. A fight now would only piss us both off even more. "Good," I said at last, figuring she'd get snarky if I kept up the Ben-trademarked silence.

She took another deep breath and used the knuckles on one hand to rub her temples. "As a woman and a mother, however, I know what sort of trouble you can get into placing yourself in a position of weakness with a man. Any man—I'm not speaking specifically of Benedikt here. Going off with a man on a date is one of the times when you are vulnerable to assault: sexual, physical, and mental."

"I've already told you," I said, deliberately keeping my voice calm. "Ben and I aren't going to have sex. He's not going to physically or mentally assault me because I'm his Beloved. That means he pretty much can't, even if he wanted to, which he doesn't."

Mom flinched at the word "Beloved" but didn't say anything about it. "There are such things as date rape, honey. There are drugs that men can give girls to knock them out so they can rape them." I started to open my mouth to protest Ben's innocence in anything so ridiculous, but she raised a hand. "No, hear me out. I know you don't think that any of this will ever happen to you, and goddess only knows I pray that it doesn't. But I want you to be prepared for any sort of attack on you, no matter whom it's from."

I bit my lip to keep from telling her I could take care of myself. She reached behind and grabbed a small bag, pulling a couple items from it.

"This," she said, holding up a small black cannister, "is pepper spray. It won't cause any permanent damage, but it should slow down anyone who attacks you."

I took the pepper spray without comment. I had actually kind of wanted some before, but never had the need for it.

"This is a Green Tara amulet." Mom held up a chain with a small stone amulet hanging from it. She slipped it over my head. I held the stone amulet up so I could see it—it was a woman who sat lotus style, kind of like a female version of Buddha. "It is warded and spelled for protection. It should keep you safe from any being from the dark powers. Keep it on you at all times. And last . . ." She pulled out of a long leather case a big herkin' knife. "If the pepper spray and Green Tara aren't enough to stop someone, this should. I don't condone violence against others, as you know, but self-protection does not fall under those precepts."

"OK," I said, pushing the knife away when she shoved it at me. "The pepper spray I'll take because it's cool. The green Buddha lady I'll take too, because it will make you happy. But I am not going to walk around with the equivalent of a sword on me!"

"Fran, it's for your own—"

"I know," I said, standing up. "And I appreciate it. The

first two are fine. I won't let Ben slip me any pills, not that he would. I won't go into a dark alley with anyone. And I won't get in any strangers' cars, OK? Are you done? It's almost six, and I have to get changed for the palm reading, so I can end early and get ready for my date."

She wasn't done, of course, but I didn't wait for her to finish before I got dressed for my time at the palm reading table. She continued to warn me right up to the moment I left the trailer.

"Mom, it's just a date, one little date, not the end of the world," I said as I opened the door and started down the stairs. She stood in the doorway giving me the same worried look she'd been giving me for the last half hour. "Stop worrying. Everything is under control, OK? Nothing bad is going to happen."

"Women and children to the hills!" Finnvid yelled as he raced by, clad in his original Viking outfit of leather and wool, his huge shining sword in one hand as he ran for the beach. "*Anfall! Anfall!* Every man to arms, we're under attack by the Vangarians. To Valhalla!"

"Except, of course, if the Vikings Eirik called for help attack us instead," I said with a lame smile.

Mom just stared.

CHAPTER FOURTEEN

"How bad is it?"

Eirik looked over his shoulder at me. He was half-hidden behind a rock, shouting orders to his men as they took up defensive positions. "Goddess Fran, you should not be here. Go back to your camp."

"Weren't these guys supposed to be helping you with Loki?" I peered over the rock at the five boats that were bobbing up and down on the waves, about twenty yards off shore. "Are those whatchamacallit . . . dragon ships?"

Eirik rolled his eyes for a moment before snatching up a walkie-talkie and barking an order into it. "You have seen too many movies. Those are long boats, traditional Viking ships. Yes, we called the Vangarians to help us, but evidently they were jealous when they heard how you took us shopping, and now they wish to pillage our many fine possessions."

An arrow whizzed past us with an odd humming noise.

"Arrow," Ljot said helpfully as he trotted past us, an air horn in one hand, a paint ball gun in the other.

I closed my eyes for a minute. "Please tell me you're not going to let them get past you to the Faire."

"No, of course not," Eirik said, shooting me an irritated glance. "There are only twenty-five of them. We will take them easily."

The walkie-talkie came to staticky life again. Eirik listened intently for a minute, then answered in Swedish.

"Good, because if there is one more incident, I don't think Absinthe is going to be very happy. Crap, I'm late. I'll check on you later to see how things are going."

"Enjoy your date. We will be here with Loki when you return," Eirik said, sticking a knife between his teeth as he grabbed his sword and leaped over the rock to race down to where the long boats were landing.

I shook my head and hustled back to the Faire, wondering for the umpteenth time why things never seemed to go easily for me.

An hour later I was in the middle of explaining to a woman that I was not responsible for her hand saying she was going to have three kids when a man jumped up on my reading table and cut off my head.

Or rather, he tried to.

"Hey!" I yelled as the sword swung straight for me. I threw up my hands to protect myself, only realizing as he started a second swing that I could partially see through him. I narrowed my eyes at the Viking. "I don't recognize you. You're not one of Eirik's men, are you? I bet you're one of those Varangians he called. Will you stop swinging that sword through me? It's annoying!"

There were three people in line behind the woman seated at my table. All four people stared in amazement as the Viking ghost turned toward them. He was dressed similarly to Eirik and his men in that he had a bare chest, wore a bit of fur strapped around his back, and had cloth pants tied on with leather leggings, but unlike my Vikings, he was partially translucent. I took it to mean he wasn't grounded the way the local ghosts were.

The people in line gasped as the Viking ghost flung himself off the table to race into the crowds wandering up around the Faire. A couple of people shrieked as he tried to behead one person, disembowel another, and hack to bits a goth guy and girl with matching face piercings, but most people applauded. Just like with Eirik and his men the previous day, the visitors thought the Vikings were part of the GothFaire performers.

"I'm sorry, I'm going to have to close early," I told the people waiting for me to read their palms. "We're having a bit of a problem with our . . . er . . . Vikings. Sorry. I should be here again tomorrow night."

Two more strange Vikings raced down the aisle, screaming what I assumed were Viking war cries, trying to kill as many people with their phantom swords as they could.

"Fabulous special effects," I heard one guy say in an English accent. "Straight out of Hollywood. Are they holograms, do you think?"

"Have to be," his friend answered, watching curiously as one of the Viking ghosts stabbed a sword into his body a couple of times. "Bloody good ones, too. I wonder where the projectors are?"

"Top of the light poles," I lied, pointing to the nearest tall stand of lights that lit the aisle.

"Ah." Both men nodded. I spied a familiar, much more solid-looking Viking, and ran to intercept him. "Isleif, what's going on? I thought you guys were going to hold your buddies at the beach?"

"They're not grounded," he answered, slinging his bow over his shoulder. "We are. We can't stop them any more than they can hurt us."

"Oh, for heaven's sake . . . what are we going to do?"

"Ref and Gils and I are trying to round them up. Once we have them together, Eirik can tell them about our plan to battle Loki. They'll like that. We'll summon Loki then, and hold him for after your date."

My date was beginning to look like it would never happen. "How are guys who can't interact physically with us going to help you with Loki?"

"He's a god," Isleif said, yelling something and pointing in the direction of the last two Viking ghosts as Gils ran by. "Gods have a presence in both the spirit and mortal worlds. An ungrounded ghost can touch him."

In the distance, a horn sounded.

"Oh, great, now what's that?" I asked, glaring at a ghost as he paused long enough to try to cut off my legs.

Isleif tipped his head to the side as he listened to the fading horn blast. "More Vangarians."

"More? No! We have enough!"

"I'd best go help Eirik," Isleif said, spinning around. "Things could get ugly if everyone decides not to cooperate."

"All right, all of you, stop it," I yelled, clapping my hands together in hopes the ghosts would pay attention to me. It was a hopeless. "You there, in the leopard skin—knock it off! Stop stabbing people."

Desdemona burst out of her booth directly on front of me, her eyes wild. The leopard print ghost looked at her as she went racing off toward the trailers.

"Well, OK, you can stab her. But leave the tourists alone!"

The Viking grinned and dashed off after Desdemona.

Ben! I yelled, desperate for some support.

He didn't answer for a couple of seconds. *What's wrong, Fran? Is your mother giving you another lecture?*

She did that earlier. It's the Viking ghosts! They're running amok!

I'll talk to Eirik, he said.

No, not those ghosts . . . these ones are friends of theirs. Or enemies, I'm not sure. They're not grounded so they can't do anything physically, but they're running around the Faire trying to kill everyone and attracting attention, and any minute now Absinthe is going to notice—

"Francesca!" a familiar female voice tinged with a German accent bellowed. I twitched.

Too late. Where are you? What are you doing?

I was having dinner, he said wryly. I had a moment of squirminess as I realized what that meant, but his choice of food wasn't of concern at the moment. *I'm on my way to help you.*

Thanks. We're going to need it.

"Vhat is going on vith your ghosts?" Absinthe demanded as she stormed toward me. "Did I not tell you to make them stop these behaviors? They are bothering the customers!"

"I'm sorry, these aren't really my ghosts, they're . . . uh . . . friends. We're trying to get them contained, but—"

At that moment, a pack of women on motorcycles roared onto the fairgrounds. They didn't stop at the parking area; they went right through it and into the center aisle.

"Fran!" A woman riding double on the first motorcycle leaned out and waved. Imogen wore a helmet, but I recognized her even through the smoky faceplate. She plucked the helmet off and smiled broadly. "Look who I found for you!"

The first motorcycle came to a stop directly in front of Absinthe and me. The woman riding it nodded at me. "I understand from Imogen that you need some help with lost warriors?"

"Er . . ." I looked from the blond woman—about six foot three inches tall, taller than me even!—to Imogen.

"This is Gunn," Imogen said, introducing her friend. "She's a Valkyrie."

"Oh! Excellent! I was wondering how to get ahold of you guys."

Gunn nodded. "We were at a resort in San Tropez having a little retreat, but Imogen convinced us this was an emergency. Where are the warriors?"

"Valkyries?" Absinthe asked, looking as all the other ladies on motorcycles pulled up. "You bring to my Faire the Valkyries?"

Five Vikings chased a group of tourists past us.

"Valkyries," Gunn said, turning to her sisters in arms. She pointed to the tourist-chasing ghosts. "Warriors!"

I won't say I'll never see a stranger sight than ancient female Nordic gods in leather jackets and spike-heeled boots riding motorcycles, chasing down equally ancient Nordic ghosts, but it was something I won't forget in a very long time. The Valkyries didn't have any trouble grabbing the Viking ghosts as they zoomed in and out of the crowds, picking off the ghosts. They just reached out, grabbed, and did an odd little shake that dissolved the ghosts into nothing. Most of the tourists were clumped together in groups watching, applauding and cheering every time one of the ghosts was snagged.

"What are they doing?" I asked.

"Sending them to Valhalla," Gunn answered.

Imogen, who had taken Absinthe aside and was explaining to her what was going on, turned to beam at me. "Am I not the cleverest person ever to find Gunn and the Valkryies to take care of the problem? Now you will not need Loki's help."

Except, of course, I wanted Loki in my power so I could force him to give me Tesla.

"Brilliant," I said, summoning a smile I didn't particularly feel. I wouldn't hurt Imogen's feelings for the world.

"Now," Gunn said, turning to me. "While they are taking care of the Vangarians, why don't you take me to the group Imogen told me about. We'd like to get back to our resort as quickly as possible. There's to be a wet T-shirt contest tonight that I just know my girls can win."

Gunn looked down at her chest fondly for a moment.

I blinked at her boobs. "Um . . . yeah. My Vikings are on the beach, trying to control the others so they can trap Loki, but once they're done with that—"

"Trap Loki?" Gunn yelled.

"What can I do to help?" a deep, smooth, velvety soft voice asked behind me.

"Ben!" I whirled around, smiling with relief to see him. "Nothing right now. Imogen brought the Valkyries to help with the ghosts."

He raised a dark eyebrow and looked at his sister. "I didn't know she knew how to call them."

She smiled back at him, winking. "You don't know what you can do until you try. Actually, Fran gave me the idea by summoning Freya. I called a few friends in Italy and managed to track her down, and she gave me Gunn's mobile number. I called and told her you needed help, and voilà! Instant backup!"

I opened my mouth to ask how on earth she knew that a Valkyrie would have a cell phone, but decided not to. If my Vikings could be addicted to McDonald's and use a laptop to plan battle strategy, what was so strange with Valkyries being summoned by a phone call rather than an invocation?

"My Vikings are over there, beyond the main tent, down at the beach," I said, directing Gunn to the area where I'd last seen Eirik.

"Groovy. Let's go get them," she said, propping her bike up against the lightpole. She peeled off a pair of leather gloves and marched off, Imogen in tow. Absinthe blinked a couple times, shot me a look, and hurried off in the other direction.

Ben looked at me. "Aren't you going as well?"

"Yeah, I am. It's just . . ." I bit my lower lip. Ben gently pulled it from between my teeth with a brush of his thumb.

"It's just what?"

"I almost hate to see them go. They're nice. And they've tried to help."

Ben laughed and put his hand on my back, giving me a little push forward. "You have such a soft heart. It's one of the things I admire most about you."

I sighed as we made our way through the crowds toward the beach. I knew I was being foolish—Eirik and his men *wanted* to go to Valhalla. It was only right that they should get there. "I'm glad you admire it, but it's annoying most of the time. Things matter so much . . . oh, no, now what?"

Ben and I started running when we heard three Viking horns go off simultaneously. It only took us a few minutes to reach the area on the beach where I'd last seen Eirik. Just as we were leaping over a couple of downed trees that were on the fringe of the beach, the remaining Valkyries roared up behind us, passing us and coming to a stop on the beach.

"Oh . . . bullfrogs!" I swore at the sight of the number of ungrounded ghosts milling around. The small stretch of beach was elbow-to-elbow with Viking longships, and there had to be at least a hundred ungrounded ghosts roaming around. In the center, a ring of Eirik's men stood, all of them looking at a redheaded man who was swearing up a blue streak at Gunn.

"I will not be summoned this way! You have no right to call me here now, and for that, you will pay!"

"Oh, blow it out your butt," Gunn said.

Loki's mouth hung open for a moment.

Gunn turned to Imogen and said in a lower voice, "I've always wanted to tell him that, the self-aggrandized little twit."

Loki roared in anger.

"Get over yourself already, will you?" Gunn asked. "No one is impressed. Eirik asked me to summon you, so get a grip and do whatever it is he wants so I can get my girls back to the t-shirt contest."

"Wow. Tough chick," I said in an undertone to Ben.

"They have to be. They're warriors, too, remember."

"Yeah. I just wish she wasn't pissing off Loki. I'm going to have a hard enough time to get him to hand over Tesla as is."

I'm here with you, he said, making me feel almost invincible. *Would you like me to deal with Loki for you?*

No, it's my problem. Tibolt gave me the valknut, so I have to do this, but thank you for asking and not just going ahead and doing it.

He smiled. *You are welcome. Imogen lectured me earlier about not allowing you to grow. I am trying to give you the space you need to learn about your powers and abilities.*

Thanks. I really appreciate that. And I appreciate more you being here when I need you. I stepped forward, pushing between Isleif and Gils to enter the ring of Vikings. Gunn looked at me curiously.

Loki snarled when he saw me. "You again?"

"Yes, me again." I raised my chin and tried to look as tough as Gunn. "I want my horse back, Loki. I want him back now. In exchange, I will return to you this valknut."

Loki laughed, his voice booming back from the rocks in a horrible double echo. "You foolish mortal. What do you think you can do to force me to give you my descendant?"

I gestured toward the ring of Vikings. "My friends are here to help me take you down if you won't cooperate."

He sneered at them. "A handful of long-dead warriors. They are no match for me."

The Valkyries stepped forward, joining the Viking ring.

"Valkyries . . . bah. A bunch of women playing at being men," he snorted. Imogen grabbed Gunn as she spat out a curse and started toward Loki.

"There are also other Viking warriors here," I said, nodding at the groups of ghosts that Eirik had convinced to help him. They stood in clusters in a semi-circle around us, watching everything silently.

Loki sent them a mocking glance. "I fear no man, dead or alive. Is this all you have, mortal? You're wasting my time."

Uh oh. He doesn't seem to be worried at all, I told Ben. *I thought seeing all those Vikings would have him changing his mind.*

You made him listen to you before, he answered. *What did you do?*

I showed him the valknut. But he just seemed mad I had it more than he feared it or anything like that.

If he wants it, that means it has some power. Use it, Fran.

Use it how? I don't know how to do any of that sort of magic. I'm just a psychometrist!

It was given to you for a reason. It has power that you can use. You just have to figure out how to access it.

I pulled the valknut from beneath my top, holding it in my hand for a moment. Ben was right—it did have power. It tingled against my palm as if it was waiting to be used. "I have the *Vikingahärta*."

Loki's smile got a whole lot nastier. "But you do not know how to use it. You have twice engaged my anger, mortal. Now you will feel my wrath." He raised his hand like he was going to smite me, or do something equally godlike, but Ben stepped in front of me.

"You will have to go through me, first."

Loki laughed again. "As if a Dark One could stop me? Prepare for annhiliation."

I thought you were going to let me do things my own way? I asked, poking him on the shoulder.

There are limits to my patience. This is one of them.

I can't make him do what I want if you won't let me try, I pointed out.

And I cannot allow him to harm you. If you are dead, you won't help Tesla.

He had a point. *OK, how about this—we do it together.*

Ben didn't like that, I could feel the need within him to protect me, but he isn't my boyfriend for nothing. He pushed back that need and said simply, *Very well. We will do this together. You will attempt to barter—if he refuses or attacks, then I will take over.*

Deal.

I moved around to his side, letting my arm brush his just because I liked the feeling. "Loki Laufeyiarson," I said in a loud voice, pulling the valknut over my head and laying the chain and pendant across my palm. The tingle changed in quality, becoming more intense until it buzzed on my hand like a joybuzzer. It also grew hot, very hot, almost too hot to hold. "Return to me the horse known as Tesla, or else I will unleash your own power against you."

Loki's hand dropped from smiting position, his eyes narrowing.

Good girl. Now you have his attention.

Yeah, but what should I do to prove to him I can use this darn thing? I have no idea how to use power. I'm not a Wiccan like my mom.

Mold it, Ben advised. *Hold it and shape it, making it take the form you want, then when you're ready, fire it at Loki.*

"You don't know how to use it," Loki said, suddenly relaxing.

I looked at the pendant glowing on my hand, my arm starting to burn from the energy and heat it gave off. I gathered together all the feelings it gave me, added to it my own anger and frustration and worry about Tesla, and formed it into a giant glowing ball.

"I want my horse," I yelled, slamming the ball of energy into Loki. To my surprise, he reeled backward, his image shimmering for a few seconds. It must have taken him by surprise, too, because the look he shot me was one of sheer fury.

Excellent, Fran. That was very well done. Ben's arm slid around my waist, under the edge of my shirt, his hand warm and comforting against my skin.

"Give me Tesla," I shouted again, getting ready to slam Loki with another jolt of power.

He leaped to the side, snarling. "You believe you have won, little mortal, but you have not. You may have your horse back, but it will be at the cost I warned you of earlier. Enjoy your defeat."

The air beside Loki shimmered and seemed to twist around on itself, forming into the shape of a familiar white horse.

"Tesla!" I tried to run forward to grab him, but Ben held me back.

"Wait until Loki is gone," he said softly. "He is the trickster. It might not really be Tesla."

"I have fulfilled your demand. Give me the *Vikingahärta.*"

I didn't want to, but I had agreed to hand it over to him in exchange for Tesla. I took a few steps forward and held it out to him. "Thank you. I promise that I will take very good care of Tesla."

Loki tried to snatch the valknut from my hand, but the second his fingers touched it, it burst into flames.

"Häxa!" he screamed, leaping back as I dropped it onto the sand. "You have enchanted it!"

Do I want to know what he called me?
Witch.

"No, I haven't, honest. It just did that on its own." The flames died down, leaving the valknut glowing slightly against the silvery sand.

"You have done something to it to keep me from taking it."

"I haven't! I swear!" I held up my hands to show they were empty.

"We will meet again," Loki warned, his voice low and ugly. His body started elongating, as if he was being stretched. "And I will not be nearly so merciful when we do."

He blipped out as the last of his words were spoken, just as if he was a picture on the TV someone had turned off. The air was heavy with his words, however, leaving a grim feeling. I ignored it, hurrying forward to Tesla, not absolutely sure he wasn't just an illusion.

He wasn't. Tesla nickered softly and rubbed his head on me, searching for apples. I blinked back a couple of happy tears, hugging his neck and rubbing my face in his mane for a moment to reassure myself that he was real.

"Thank you," I said finally, turning to face the Vikings, Valkyries, and ghosts that had gathered to help me. "Thank you all so much. I can't tell you how much it means to me to have Tesla back."

My Vikings grinned. "We were happy to help, goddess, although sad we could not disembowl Loki," Eirik said. "Perhaps you are having trouble with another god?"

I shook my head. "No. Everything's fine now. Thank you. I'm going to miss you guys. I hope you enjoy Valhalla. Gunn?"

She stepped forward, waving her warrior sisters on as well. "Absolutely. Valkyries! We have warriors to escort!"

The Vikings smiled. In less time than it took to say

smorgasbord, the beach was empty of everything but one white horse, Imogen, Ben, and me.

"I hope they got to take their stuff with them to Valhalla," I said, stroking Tesla's neck. His eyes were half closed as he leaned into the petting. He looked fine, not like he'd been overworked or underfed. His coat was shiny and and clean, and someone had worked a few braids into his tail and mane. "I can't believe it, but I'm going to miss them."

"They have gone on to their reward," Imogen said, consoling me. She patted me on the shoulder and even gave Tesla's ears a quick rub. "They will be happy. I shall miss Finnvid greatly, but I am pleased for them. And for you, too, Fran. That took much bravery, facing Loki as you did. I am very proud of you."

"Thanks," I said, giving her a quick hug. "I couldn't have done it if you hadn't brought the Valkyries."

"Pfft," she said, waving a hand. "You didn't need them. You would have simply made Loki send the Vikings on first. Ah well, it has been an interesting evening." She sent Ben a little smile. "And I'm sure it will become even more interesting. I'll see you both later."

"You're awfully quiet," I told Ben, looking at him over Tesla's neck. He stood in the same spot, not moving, not saying anything, just watching me with dark, black eyes. "Is it because I didn't thank you yet for helping me? I was going to do that later, on our date."

"No," he said, and for a second, I felt a wave of concern and worry come from him.

"What's wrong?"

"What exactly were Loki's words to you the first time

you summoned him? When you refused to give him the valknut?"

I glanced over to where the valknut laid innocently on the sand. It was cool to the touch. With nothing else to do with it but leave it—something I didn't want to do—I slipped it back over my head next to the Green Tara, and thought back a couple days. "He said that if I didn't return it, he would take that which I most valued. But that is you, and you're standing here, fine as can be. In fact, everything is fine. The Vikings have been sent on to Valhalla, Tesla is back, and there's still time for us to go on our date. I'd say things are looking up for a change."

Ben gave me an odd look. "Fran—" he started to say, but was interrupted by a shout from Soren at the edge of the beach.

"Fran! Benedikt! You must come! Something terrible has happened."

A chill rippled down my back and arms as I grabbed Tesla and urged the horse into a trot.

"What's wrong? Are there more Vikings? We can call the Valkyries back—"

"No, it is not them," Soren said, turning as we reached him. "It's the troll."

I stopped dead in my tracks. "The *what?*"

Soren grabbed my sleeve in order to drag me to the other side of the island. "A troll. It kind of looks like a wrinkled-up TV actress. He says he's looking for the goddess who sent the Vikings on to Valhalla because he wants to be released as well. You'd better come quickly before he gets annoyed. He's already talking about making you take him shopping first."

I took a deep breath and shot a glance at Ben.

He looked at me without expression for a minute, then burst into laughter, wrapping his arm around me and pulling me up close. "Ah, Fran. I can see life with you is going to be anything but dull."

AUTHOR'S NOTE

I took a lot of poetic license with my interpretation of Viking ghosts, and Nordic gods, but I hope that devotees of Nordic history will forgive any trespasses. If you have a comment you'd like to make about that, or anything else in the book or series, feel free to e-mail me. Links to my e-mail and mailing address can be found on my website (www.katiemaxwell.com).

And finally, I'd like to thank my friend Tobias Barlind for answering my endless questions about Sweden, Vikings, and providing translations. No matter what time of day I asked him for help, no matter how strange the request (and how many people have the opportunity to translate the phrase "legless weasel"— the name of the nearby town in *Circus of the Darned?*), Tobias always came through for me. *Tack så mycket,* Tobias.

Didn't want this book to end?

There's more waiting at **www.smoochya.com**:

Win FREE books and makeup!
Read excerpts from other books!
Chat with the authors!
Horoscopes!
Quizzes!